STEDFAST

STEDFAST
GUARDIAN ANGEL

ROGER ELWOOD

WORD PUBLISHING
Dallas·London·Vancouver·Melbourne

STEDFAST
Copyright © 1992 Roger Elwood

Library of Congress Cataloging-in-Publication Data

Elwood, Roger
    Stedfast : guardian angel / Roger Elwood.
        p.   cm.
    Third vol. of the author's Angelwalk saga trilogy; the first is
Angelwalk and the second is Fallen Angel.
        ISBN 0–8499–3240–8
        I. Title.
    PS3555.L85S74   1992
    813'.54—dc20   91–47092
                                                       CIP

Printed in the United States of America

2 3 4 5 6 7 8 9 LBM 7 6 5 4 3 2 1

To Gigi and Boy-Boy
who could teach
the hardest of hearts
what love and devotion
are all about

Human beings are promised a Heaven without tears, without pain . . . but that is not the case for angels. It is something that we have become accustomed to waiting for, an anticipated blessing that will be ours when we all experience the new Heaven and the new earth.

We regularly journey to the present earth, the earth so pitiably torn by Satan's ravaging presence, and spend a brief time there—or longer, if we are particularly brave—and then we must return to Heaven with the bleak and tragic baggage from that sojourn weighing us down, for we cannot tolerate what Satan has done with the planet. We feel a desperate need to engage in the spiritual equivalent of taking a bath. And that is what we do, as we stand before the Father and let His purity cleanse us . . . until the next time.

Holy, Holy, Holy, that day when there is no more next time, when we do not have to brace ourselves for the battles that now take place on Planet Earth and in the heavenlies. Wonderful it shall be, and ready my kind and I are.

—STEDFAST

Acknowledgments

THE YEAR WAS 1988.

I had decided to leave all secular career pursuits, and turn my time totally over to Jesus Christ. For one thing, I would no longer edit any non-Christian science fiction, since the whole direction of that genre had become increasing nihilistic or pantheistic or atheistic or any number of other -istics that happened to be popular at the time. I would interview no more celebrities, except for the Christian media, I would focus no more attention upon the wrong role models for young people, to name one age group. Thus, I would cease involvement with any pursuit not anchored in a Christ-centered perspective.

Today. . . .

Now a number of years later.

The book that was used so dramatically by the Lord, in 1988, to solidify the change in my direction led to a successful sequel, a number of other books, some awards, and a great deal of media exposure.

Judging by the sales figures and the majority of the reviews, the Christian reading public is more than a little receptive to fiction that tackles subjects more serious than fluffy romances.

I even received a letter from an officer who was involved in Operation Desert Storm; he had read most of my books, and was pleased that someone had encouraged him, through fiction, to *think*. He shared each one with his buddies, and found the novels to be an effective witnessing tool.

I owe an enormous debt to Joey Paul at Word, perhaps more than to any other individual. He enabled me to write *Fallen Angel* and *Stedfast* as I really wanted to do, in a way that would maximize Christ-centered truths and address issues that other publishers might not have allowed. He is the best possible kind of editor, the greatest with whom I have been privileged to work over a twenty-seven-year career, for Joey allows a writer to do what that writer hopefully does best—*write*. I feel as though Joey and I are brothers as well as editor-writer, and I would be happy indeed if we continued our association for a lifetime.

There are many others—Warren Wiersbe, Harold Lindsell, Jess Moody—who have been so very helpful over the years.

God bless them all.

ROGER ELWOOD

Introduction

STEDFAST IS THE THIRD *ANGELWALK* BOOK, the second sequel.

It is different in many ways from *Angelwalk* and *Fallen Angel*, though Stedfast was a character in both of the previous books.

But then Stedfast is different, as well. Whereas Darien of *Angelwalk* was a questioning, somewhat rebellious angel while remaining essentially unfallen, and Observer of *Fallen Angel* was an altogether demonic angel, yet a quite reluctant one in the long run, Stedfast is neither questioning nor fallen. He is one of the elite corps of angels, if I may put it that way, always steady, always serving the Trinity, always perfectly obedient and faithful with not even a thought out of place.

Legends are often born from nuggets of truth during the course of earthly history. And Stedfast, according to the *mythos* of this series, was the origin of the legend of the Guardian Angel.

He is wiser than Darien. Ah, he is certainly that! He knows the answers to the questions for which Darien was searching in *Angelwalk*.

Steady as a rock. . . .

That's Stedfast, for sure.

But this angel is also one with an enormous capacity to assimilate the feelings of every creature with which he comes in contact, their emotions his own, to a real and vivid extent.

He is a sponge, this Stedfast.

And he yearns for the day when, like redeemed humans, he will know only the joy, the peace of Heaven.

Without the tears that only the angels, only the Trinity will continue to shed until then. . . .

This indeed is a striking truth. The Creator weeps in Heaven; His human creations do not. For divinity, there is sorrow, there is anguish. But flesh-and-blood beings who have accepted Jesus Christ as Savior and Lord have been promised freedom, forever, from such as this.

We have to wait for our full participation in that same promise, unfallen angelkind and I among them.

Until the new Heaven, the new earth, that wondrous trans-formation toward which all of history is heading.

That is when we shed our own veil of tears, and walk together in the special sunlight of that special day, never again looking back, the past washed away in a flood of eternal joy. . .

Stedfast's Prologue

I t is going to be soon. The ethereal fabric of Heaven itself hums and buzzes and flashes with anticipation.

That Moment. . . .

Oh my, what can I do? How can I face it without embarrassing myself and the rest of my kind by emotion unstoppable?

That Moment for which we all have been waiting—how indeed we have been waiting for it to arrive! Countless have been our entreaties before the Trinity as we bow in humble adoration, but also with our incessant petitions, again and again—and been told over and over, "Not as yet, dear ones. Not as yet."

So we turn away, perhaps to welcome another soul past the Gates, perhaps to leave that place of wonder and joy altogether on a mission of one sort or another, or simply to sit beside a crystal lake and think back over what has been, the sum total of our existence until—

That Moment.

Oh, blessed Jesus, it is soon. It is going to happen soon. We will no longer be leaving Heaven to stride in our obedience across continents of bloodshed and fear, of crime and disease, of sin in every form devised by the fleshly nature of Humankind.

Soon it will be that we will visit instead the new earth, cleansed and reborn, just as the faithful have been, and we will walk hand in hand back to Eden.

Oh my . . . .

But then, in the interlude before that odyssey begins, as I sit here beside the crystal lake, preparing myself for what I will say to the gathered multitudes, human and angelic alike, awaiting that which has been prophesied, I think back, so far back, so long ago, and I shiver, yes, I shiver as bits and pieces present themselves to me . . . .

Their souls cry out, you know.

The damned always do that as they are taken to Hell. They could have been in the company of angels, but they chose other companions instead.

They cry a great deal.

That is what I hear most of all. More than the gnashing of teeth.

The sound of their weeping, their tears.

Tears do speak in a certain way, if you listen carefully— not with words, certainly not that, but in other respects.

Forgive me, please, for being vague with this. I am so because the *sensation* of which I speak is not altogether definable, nor easily so.

It is a feeling, I suppose . . . .

Yes, that may be the best answer, if not a satisfactory one.

My comrades and I were not created bereft of feelings, you know. We have them, my fellow angels and I. We have our own, and we also experience the feelings of every being with which we come in contact.

When they, the mortal ones, the ones of flesh and blood and bone and marrow, are evil, when they are held often inextricably in the sway of sin, the feelings born from them tend to be repugnant. In this we get a hint of what Hell is like, a hint that is, by itself, enough to make us so very glad that we chose Jehovah the Almighty instead of Lucifer the Magnificent.

And yet any allegiance won purely by fear is tenuous at best, for the one feared the most can always be replaced by another of more fearsome intent. But it was not so with us, the unfallen. We have loved our Lord and Him only. We would *gladly* go into Hell itself if He only asked.

Did Lucifer?

Love Him, ever?

It cannot be said that Lucifer did, *truly*—oh, perhaps, after his own fashion, for the first few thousand years or so, or their equivalent, before the Casting-Out. But after that, which is but a small portion of eternity, his *desires* overtook him, desires that made him jealous of everything that God could do, everything He was, everything indeed.

. . . *everything He was.*

But Lucifer forgot the love part, forgot the kindness, forgot all but the *power* of God.

"I want what He has," I overheard the loveliest of all of us saying. "I want His throne! I want to *rule!*"

He approached me as I stood in a quiet place.

"Stedfast, I *need* you," Lucifer purred, exuding all the charm of which he was capable, for his countenance had not as yet suffered the devastating corruption of his deeds.

How glorious this angel was, a face of great magnificence, like the finest sculpture ever done by man during the height of the Renaissance.

"I will not," I replied.

"But you will be always in subservience to *Him*," Lucifer continued, astonished that I could resist what a third of the other angels had committed to in His presence.

"And not to *you?*" I scoffed. "You ask me not to choose freedom, which you pretend to offer, but, rather, between two masters. If it is a slave that I am destined to be, then I must follow in the steps of the greater of the two."

He waited, thinking that, surely, this meant him.

"Oh, my friend, my friend," I said to Lucifer upon realizing this. "Can you not now see . . . ?"

He could not. He was lost by then. He had become the captive of his own passions.

I looked at Lucifer with great pity.

"Goodbye . . . " I said.

"You will miss me, Stedfast," he replied. "You know that. You will wish you had gone on with me to victory."

This magnificent being raised a glowing hand, not yet devoid of its glory, now doubled into a fist.

"There will be a point," Lucifer said, smiling, "at which you—"

He lowered that hand, his body shivering ever so slightly.

"Why am I so cold?" he said out loud, undoubtedly regretting the momentary vulnerability this lent him.

"Judgment," I told him. "You have felt a taste of it already."

"Nonsense!" he screamed.

Our Father which art in Heaven.

We both heard that chorus.

"Why are they *doing* that?"

"They are singing a song of triumph."

"But I recognize it not."

"It has not been written as yet. It has not been spoken as yet. It resides only in the mind of the King of kings and Lord of lords."

Lucifer clutched his temple.

"You have not yet broken the bond," I told him. "It is still there, your mind and God's connected."

"No! I will not be a mere extension of Him any longer!"

The rage of that cry echoed throughout the Heavenly Kingdom.

And lead us not into temptation but deliver us from evil. For thine is the kingdom, and the power, and the glory forever. . . .

Lucifer was granted that which he wished. The bond between him and Almighty God was broken.

We all felt it. For a moment there was a hint of darkness in Heaven, transitory but chilling, though we and the Trinity alone felt it, human souls to be insulated from such for eternity.

Lucifer started to change in appearance even then, the glory that once had been his and his alone amongst us suddenly dimming and something else taking its place, something foul and perverse.

Sin.

Sin was separation from God, a death of communion with Him.

Lucifer had sinned. Along with ten thousand upon ten thousand of my once fellow angels.

They were finally leaving.

"I will be back," he shouted, "to storm the gates!"

Lucifer turned for the last time and saw us there, saw our sorrow, saw the tears.

"Weep not for us," he roared with defiance. "Rather, weep for *yourselves*. Realize what lies in store as I gain control over that planet which Jehovah created with such hope, and along with it, the rest of the universe. I will take that hope and destroy it forever!"

The horde of them, now screeching, loathsome *things* consumed by their own vile natures, that horde fell to the world below, and beyond, to the pit of another place, a new place, a place created for the damned and by the damned . . . like themselves.

And that is their story.

Feelings . . . .

We are the only creations of God to experience such feelings of darkness in the midst of His holy Heaven, you know.

We do that because we regularly journey between Heaven and earth. Those human beings who have accepted Christ as Savior and Lord and who have been allowed into Heaven as a result are shielded from the pain of earth, the dying of earth—yes, even the tears.

My angel-kin and I all await the moment when we will experience the same kind of peace. But we do not know it just now. For us, there is little solace so long as we trod the path called Angelwalk. For each of us has his own Angelwalk, which is as much a name for the very journey itself.

Angelwalk . . . .

It is a path of pain, a path of joy—it is both of these and more.

It is the story of Darien, my fellow angel, with all his uncertainties, with his quest to piece together the reality of Satan for himself.

Another story is mine. I had no doubts, you see no uncertainties. Nor did Michael. Or Gabriel.

Another story indeed . . . .

We take our feelings with us when we journey to earth, and we take them back with us when we report to the Trinity.

We stand before the Throne, and we weep. We weep for the lost. We know what God intended for the planet, and we weep over what it has become. We beg Him not to send us back—surely, we will not have to return, surely we can instead continue to stand amidst the cleansing atmosphere of Heaven itself and be washed pure again, without going back to the dirt below.

Surely . . . .

God cries, too.

Oh, He does. Jesus truly wept in human form. That did not end the moment the Son of God ascended. This capability was with Him before the Incarnation. It remains today.

We often serve to help the blessed Comforter, and we do our best, mostly when humans are in pain, when we can step into their lives and stay by their sides. We cannot hold their hands, of course. We cannot rub their foreheads. We cannot put our arms around their frail bodies and sing to them. But we do more, much more, you see.

This, then, is my story, which I recount now as I stand in front of Father, Son, and Holy Spirit, and before all those created beings, human and angelic alike, who have remained loyal, loving followers of the Most High. It would not surprise me if some scribe is quietly marking down what I say, to be put in some form on the shelf of a majestic new library somewhere.

I know I cannot delay any longer, for as soon as I finish, I shall join these the residents of the Kingdom as we all begin the long anticipated journey triumphant from the new Heaven to the new earth, all things new, forever and ever . . . .

The Odyssey

*E*very seat is taken.

On stage at the front of the auditorium are only two individuals, a fragile-looking boy and his mother. Even though the loudspeaker is on full blast, the child's words sometimes are difficult to hear.

"I am very tired now," he says, and rests his head on his mother's shoulder, and dies.

She continues to stand there, though she is obviously trying to fight back tears that are beginning to drip over her lower lids and down her cheeks.

Suddenly there is the sound of voices raised in prayer. The hundreds of men and women in that auditorium stand and—

I see Heaven opening up.

I see angels descending. They stand around little Robbie as his soul begins to leave his body.

They are waiting, I know, waiting for me, waiting for me to do that which has been ordained. And I know, how blessed it is, I know what I must do. I must take that soul, pure and healthy from that diseased and now dead flesh, I must lift it from corruption and give it to incorruption.

Something quite wonderful happens. Words come from the soul of a child, words without pain, words of sublime joy.

"Peace like a river attendeth my way . . . . "

Robbie starts to sing that remembered hymn, and the gathered angels join him, sharing its wonderful lyrics as none who were still trapped in their fleshly bodies could ever do, could ever do with the same meaning.

And that expression on Robbie's face! Peace envelopes him, as water surrounded the baptized Jesus in the River Jordan. All that is finite, all that was born to perish, has passed away.

In an instant, the Holy Spirit descends not as a dove—no need of symbols or surrogates any longer.

I hand Robbie to Him—a brave and beautiful child, now glistening, now cleansed—I hand this precious one to this Member of the Trinity. The Holy Spirit looks at me for a moment, smiles, and I feel His radiance throughout my very being. He smiles, yes, and He says, "You will miss him while you are here, will you not?"

"Oh, I will, I will," I admit, incapable as I am of lies, deception.

"You were with him for so long, and now you will wait expectantly for the reunion, is that not so, Stedfast?"

"Yes," I agree. "He was so fine, this child. He smiled in the midst of pain. He never became angry. He stayed faithful even as the disease ravaged him more and more severely. If I were of flesh and blood, he is the son I would want, I would pray for."

The Holy Spirit, touched by my words, says, "The Father knows. He knows, and He rejoices because of you."

I have brought joy to my Creator! I have pleased Almighty God!

"It is time now," the Holy Spirit says as He turns to the child. "Robbie, are you ready?"

Robbie nods eagerly and reaches out toward me.

"Thank you, Stedfast," he tells me. "I prayed to Jesus about you every night. I thanked Him for sending such a beautiful angel to be with me. The pain didn't hurt as much because I could feel your presence, and nothing else mattered, Stedfast. God bless you, God bless you, dear, dear angel, angel of mercy, angel of joy."

I try to control myself though barely managing to do so.

Robbie casts a glance at the crowd in that auditorium. They had come to the Christian media convention to buy and sell. They had come to hear speeches. And none would ever be the same again after listening to what his mother had to say of her struggle to save the life of this her beloved son.

Voices are now raised in praise, many present with their palms upheld. Though none can actually see what is happening, they can somehow sense the presence of divinity. This child, now free, now whole, reaches out toward them and in a beautiful way touches each one with his gentle and good spirit, some driven to tears as they fall to their knees.

Robbie hesitates but an instant as he looks at his mother that final, final moment before, someday, they walk the golden streets together. Her tears have formed a river of their own.

"I love you, " he whispers. "I love you so much, dearest Mother."

Not words at all, at least as far as she or any of them can perceive.

A sensation.

Something rippling in the air, perhaps, gossamerlike.

She senses it instinctively, raising her head toward the ceiling—and at the same moment there is a touch of concern, a last fleeting reluctance to let go, to acknowledge her beloved's odyssey.

"It is well with my soul, Mother," I can hear Robbie say clearly. "I see Jesus waiting, you know. He says He will take your hand, too, Mother, and very soon. Don't be afraid. My Lord, your Lord loves you as much as I do."

And then Robbie is gone.

His mother smiles as she raises the fingers of her left hand to her lips, kisses these, and holds them out to the empty air.

"He is not there, sweet lady," I say. "He is beyond the Gates now. His feet touch streets of gold. His ears listen to the songs of angels. There are so many gathering around him. He is at peace, this child of yours. He is—"

Home.

Observer also was there at the time, Satan's demonic journalist, so chained to his master, yet so reluctant. Other fallen ones had urged him not to enter, for they all were leaving in a panic. There was too much faith, too much sweetness, too much love in that room, and they could not endure it.

But he stayed. And I did.

We saw the same beautiful moments. And we left that place touched by what had happened, me to the rededication of myself to the Cause of Christ, Observer back to his puppet master.

"I could do nothing to stop it," Observer told me.

"Did you want to stop it?" I asked incredulously.

"No," he admitted. "I pray that Satan will never find out."

"Would he punish you?"

"Yes. Horribly."

And I watched him go, my former comrade. I watched him go, and I remembered how it once was, before evil began . . . .

Those first wonderful days!

True and I were selected by the Trinity to help Them in the process of creation. Yes, it may seem strange to say that, for surely They need no help with such matters. But it was done not for the sake of Father, Son, and Holy Spirit. Rather, it was for True, for me. Even then we were being groomed, I realize now, groomed for special tasks and special destinies.

And there he and I were as Adam and Eve came to life, Adam from the soil, Eve from his side.

They saw us, and they smiled without fear.

Without fear!

Think of the wonder of that. It is the same awe many feel when a baby killer whale is born at one of those modern sea-life-type parks, born and swimming in an instant, as though it had been doing so forever.

Thus it was with the first humans, born out of nothingness, yet accepting us with no reluctance, no doubt over whether or not they were hallucinating, just simple faith, faith together with trust.

The destruction of this is a very large part of the foundation of my hatred for Satan.

The death of pure trust.

I find that as tragic as the death of faith, for once faith is present, trust should be, yes, *easier!* Yet without faith, trust-lessness is understandable. It cannot be transformed into what is nobler, grander. It hangs like a dark cloud, submerging all who choose to allow it to dominate every second of life.

Those who have faith and do not couple it with trust are bastard creatures, born indeed, alive and walking and *doing*—but with victory robbed from their lives, exaltation drained from the days accorded them.

Adam and Eve had it.

Adam and Eve lived it.

And we, True and I, saw it in their eyes, in their words, in the very walk of those two.

That was why they did not fear the serpent.

Later, other angels, including Darien, joined us. Later, the Garden was alive with them. And because of this, because of our radiance, there was no night. Oh, technically there was night, but we banished it by our presence. We set the Garden aglow with color, sparkling with some of the light of Heaven itself—for that was what we were made of, you know, the glow of the Creator transfused throughout His Kingdom, from which we were created by His loving Hand, as though, playfully, He would grab some of it, hold it, and then let it go as another angel beamed to life, countless thousands of us, thousands times thousands, God remarkably like an innocent child in a long-ago time on earth, a child grabbing at sparkling soap bubbles he has created—and there the comparison ends, for when a child opens his hand, he finds nothing, but when God did, He found us.

*L*ike a river glorious. . . .

There was indeed a river named Glorious in Eden, the water like molten crystal, sparkling under an overhead sun whose pure rays were not filtered through layers of pollution spewed up into the atmosphere.

There was no industry in those days.

There was no death.

There was no sin.

Like a world glorious.

That was how it used to be, you know. Adam and Eve began in Eden, but this was intended as only the start. God was prepared to take them on a wondrous journey around the world, their Guide through the wonders of a planet that was, in so many ways, a mirror image of Heaven itself, an extension of its glories. Eden was the nucleus, with everything else spreading out from it. Eden offered to this first couple a taste of what the world was like. God planned to show them the rest.

I saw what the two humans had not as yet.

I saw a world of waterfalls of liquid gold.

I saw a world of colonies of unfallen angels clustered together, chattering about what they saw around them, comparing it to their previous heavenly home, and excited about the future, for they were to be caretakers of this new place, sprung as it was from the mind of God, as they themselves had been.

There were no battles for us in Eden nor anywhere else on earth at that time, it seemed. Satan had been vanquished. We all assumed, so foolishly, our former comrade would never again reappear.

I saw a world where no living thing died in the mouth of another.

I saw a world in which a lion sat contentedly simply looking at a color-drenched butterfly going from flower to flower in a field of orchids.

I saw a world that—

—*was so much like Heaven itself!*

I said that before, I know, but it is so blessed a fact that I cannot but repeat it.

That had been the purpose, of course. God wanted His newest creations—Adam and Eve—to exist in a world of the finest elements that He could provide.

And Planet Earth was that, the very finest.

The Father intended this to be forever. If there were no death, then mankind would never die. If there were no death, then mankind never needed to eat meat. Eating involved decay of one sort or another, animal or vegetable. But with eternal life, there would have been no hunger, no thirst, cattle and geese and lobsters spared.

Funny, isn't it, how I always took pity, somehow, on the lobsters, crammed into their glass tanks as they were, then taken out and shown to the one into whose stomach bits and pieces of them would soon drop, before which the eater would examine the eatee and say, "Yes, that's a good specimen," and into the broiler it would go.

None of that in the original Eden.

I saw lobsters, yes, I saw a whole inlet of them; they were moving about rather briskly for their kind, not shackled by the need to hunt prey, and so they had no cares at all, and could live as they were meant to live, without stress, without fear.

Perhaps talking about lobsters seems inappropriate, but it is not that at all. They are hardly of a shape and a look that engenders any degree of affection. Yet in the world of that Edenic period, they were as well cared for as any creature on the planet. It was not by appearance that they were accorded what they enjoyed but the very fact that they *were,* period, that they *existed,* that the least in God's Kingdom had all the respect of the greatest—except for man.

I saw this world in all its wonders. And I craved the day, still hence, when I could join the Father, and assist Him as we walked with Adam and Eve, sharing it with them, their guides through the most miraculous journey either of them would ever have.

For since death had not as yet entered the world, so it was that they were aware of the angels around about them. So it was that I, Stedfast, joined with them to be one of their guardians—the other a dear comrade named True.

And so it was that they were aware of us. Sin would change that. Sin would establish a barrier between us, between all humans and all angels. Future humans would talk about us, would write poems and songs about us, would speculate about us in books—but with no memory of what it once was like.

We were torn from Adam and Eve, and they from us.

That day came as a chill breeze through a graveyard, unexpected, making us shiver at the consequences.

A bright world, a world of seamless purity torn from eternal light into abysmal darkness.

Darien had left to do the Creator's bidding elsewhere, but I remained, along with True. We tried to dissuade Adam and Eve, to whisper into their ears, to stop them in some way or another.

We could not *physically* do anything. Even then we were spirits only, a breeze against the cheek, an insubstantial sensation, but not more than that.

We lost.

We lost that first battle, and, thus, began the war.

That has stayed with me through the centuries since, the thousands of years of separation from God that have dominated history's walk.

We lost that first battle . . . .

All of mankind has suffered because we weren't strong enough, our words like puffs of cotton, easily waved aside, when they should have been heavy weights pressing down Adam and Eve in constraint.

Those first moments after Adam and Eve were cast from Eden are not chronicled in Scripture. Nor have I found them so anywhere in all the literature of man.

But I know them. I knew them then. I know them now. They are fresh in my thoughts, and will not be exorcised until the new Heaven, the new earth.

To have that awful time wiped from memory will be one of the Father's greatest blessings.

To no longer witness in recollection—oh, please, let it be soon, dear Father—death rushing in, animals not accustomed to pain suddenly consumed with it, many dying in their tracks, creatures large and small, creatures of the air and the sea and the land, all gasping or groaning or shaking their lives away.

And we, my friend True and I, could do nothing.

Oh, how worthless I felt at such times of remembering how we failed, trying to reconstruct in my mind what it had been like in Eden back then, those moments of communion, flesh aware of spirit, spirit understood by flesh—communion, yes, but also connection, *angels and humans as almost a single entity, an interweaving of one with the other.*

Joined.

Oh, yes, we were, Stedfast with Adam and True with Eve.

Stedfast and True—we were the angels with the most precious assignment of all, to be with the first human beings. We were their companions, their friends. How cherished those moments were, blessed and—

Missed.

Having tasted all that was fulfilling to us and pleasing to the Father, we could not have been less prepared for the expulsion of Adam and Eve.

To be joined together in holy matrimony.

What it was like for a man and a woman in the most ecstatic moments of their passion was very close to what True and I felt. We were "married," in a sense, to Adam and Eve. Indeed, we had the greatest possible intimacy.

Marriage, then, is yet another hint of Eden, not a relationship to be mocked by an endless repetition of marriage-divorce, marriage-divorce, marriage-divorce, a marriage license no better in such instances than the key to a cheap motel room for a night of illicit passion.

How do I describe that moment, that moment when Adam and Eve were ripped from True and myself?

True did not want to release Eve. He cried out to her, "Recant! Recant! God forgives. Please, please—!"

She did not. Nor did Adam.

They saw only their nakedness and they were ashamed.

There was something worse. While they lost Eden, they did not lose their memories of it. They would be tormented by this until the day they died, remembering the beauty, the peace, the joy of Eden, and doing this in the midst of the new world in which they found themselves, a world filled with death.

From never-ending life to always-present death.

In Eden, Adam and Eve could stand before a beautiful flower, and admire it again and again, week after week, month after month, for years at a time, knowing that nothing would ever affect that flower, its colors unceasingly vibrant, its shape always delicate, its scent forever, no disease to kill it, no hungry insects to drain away its life, no change of seasons to make it turn brittle, then fall to the ground. It was a flower made by God simply as a way of pleasing them.

It was all for them, these first two humans, a world into which the Father had placed them for their enjoyment, for their exaltation—but also for their stewardship, a stewardship that was to have been of great sensitivity and care, for this was one way they both had of returning to Him the supreme love that gave them life in the first place—that flower and many others even more masterfully-made, that lake and its pure water, the air which they took into their lungs a gift directly from God, their only obligation so simple, an obligation to appreciate His grace and goodness and generosity, to show this appreciation merely by obeying His one outright command—not a cruel one, not a command that would limit their world to any measurable degree—and yet they turned their backs on the Father, resenting the one part of the garden that was off-limits to them, where stood that one tree out of countless numbers actually more attractive than it, its fruit eclipsed in appearance by any number of others hanging from trees to either side of it—but it was the only small requirement that God had, the one simple test to which He put them. And thus went their loyalty, loyalty as filthy rags in the midst of paradise.

They were gone.

True and I stood there, side by side, watching the man and the woman as they ran into a world that showed the first encroaching signs of their foul transgression, a tiny bird having dropped from the course of its flight and landed in front of the two of them. They paused for a moment in their sudden exodus, Eve bending down, picking up the gray and white creature, not quite dead, its head turning, looking at her, then at Adam, and saying by this, *What have you done? What have you done to me, to the rest of creation?*

And then it was gone, its body cold in an instant.

Adam and Eve dug the first grave. . . .

"Goodbye, True," I told my friend.

"Goodbye, Stedfast," he replied, his brilliance dimming in his sorrow.

He turned, briefly, and looked back, and I with him, the Garden the same as at its moment of creation, as colorful and alive as ever, within its boundaries the cold, awful grip of death still vanquished. . . for the moment but not for all time.

"No one can enter," he told me. "No one can enter until the new Heaven, the new earth."

"You are to guard it until the end of time," I said.

"I shall face hordes of demons, Stedfast," he said, stating something that would have seemed incomprehensible just a short while earlier, but now had become, in human terms, a fact of life.

He was only momentarily tremulous at that thought.

"Lucifer himself shall stand before me."

"But you will remain . . . steadfast."

"Yes, oh, yes, steadfast and true," he said, smiling, reaching out to me, our spirits blending briefly, "our valor our gift back to the Father who made us all."

And then my fellow unfallen and I parted, doing so for unknowable centuries ahead of us . . . my good, good friend remaining there, alone, somehow succeeding in preventing entry, until One and only One would tell him that the time had come to stand aside, stand aside indeed, and rejoin his comrades . . . and I, Stedfast, wanting to stay, to be with him, to help in whatever fashion I could, but called by the Master of us all to minister instead to Humankind, not other angels so self-sufficient, as they were, of course, so able to stand and fight the enemy . . . but always my thoughts, though not my presence, were with this one angel, knowing all too well the multitude of loathsome monsters which were certain to confront him throughout the jumbled history of mankind, to offer him, as enticingly as possible, their own version of the forbidden fruit of Eden, in return for his doing something quite simple, that is, merely standing aside and allowing simple entry, but always this angel would be resisting, never giving in, a gentle angel, yet with the unflinching valor of a warrior and the spirit of a poet, turning back tides of evil for all of history, remaining, as ever he would, strong and brave and . . . yes, blessed friend . . . True.

I walk the centuries. I see the effects of sin more than any historian because I see them as they occur, not simply as I plow through manuscripts that turn to dust at the slightest touch.

I see it all.

Until the new Heaven and the new earth, as promised by God to human and angel alike.

But in the meantime. . . .

So much of what I have witnessed has been due to the inability of one individual to communicate fully with another. It was not that way in Eden. Adam and Eve did not need physical intimacy to become as one. They were already in total union with one another, with the Father, and with all of creation.

But they sinned, and the links were broken all around. God no longer spoke to them audibly. He did so to others in the centuries to follow, but such times were miraculous interventions rather than normal occurrences.

That first creature fell from the sky.
Cain took the life of his brother.

From that awful moment to the infamy of the Holocaust
to the mass destruction of Hiroshima and Nagasaki to the
Vietnam War to poison gas on the battlefields of Iran and Iraq
was not much of a leap, in the final analysis, because it all
sprang from the same awful abyss of mankind's rebellion
against God—that and a global allegiance to Satan, sometimes
knowingly, sometimes otherwise.

Families have been splitting apart since the earliest Old
Testament days because they did not communicate. Govern-
ments have been at war because they did not communicate. In
the latter part of the twentieth century, there seemed to be a
multitude of greater than ever *means* to effect communication, but less and less communication itself.

All of creation has suffered.

Communication is not simply *talking*. It involves understanding. There was plenty of talk before and during the
American Civil War, but nothing was accomplished until too
much blood was shed, until the South found itself losing far
too many of its men—*and then the war ended.*

There was not enough understanding that slavery was an
abomination in the sight of God. There was not enough understanding that those who claimed the name of Christ and
supported slavery were skirting blasphemy.

Once again, blood covered talk, silencing it, because understanding was the greatest casualty.

I was active during this period. I was with the North as
well as the South. I took dying Rebels and Yankees to the gates
of Heaven. I took slaves and free men.

And I watched many snatched by taloned creatures of loathsome countenance and dragged beyond the mouth of Hell.

It mattered not which side the dying were on. Any soldier fighting in defense of slavery was not guaranteed damnation because of this; any soldier fighting in opposition to slavery was not guaranteed salvation as a result.

General Lee went to Heaven.

That may be surprising to some . . . *Robert E. Lee in Heaven!*

I have not seen some quite prominent Northern generals there, men whose pulpit was a liquor bottle, the only source from which they drank, feeling no need for spiritual refreshment. Robert E. Lee was simply obeying *his* commander. What Lee did, he felt was the honorable course even though, in the end, he acknowledged that he had spent many, many nights dealing with emotions that were on the other side.

Some plantation owners are in Heaven. Slaves were, to them, well-nigh members of their family, given similar privileges. Their slaves got such food, good clothes, and medical attention that were equal to that of any white person on the plantation.

I remember one group of slaves that had fought to defend their owner's property *against* invading Northern soldiers, not because they had been ordered to do so, but out of a sense of personal loyalty, given freely, and reacting against strangers coming in and taking over.

"What could we do?" the survivors cried. "They were bent on destroying the only way of life we have ever known. For us, there had never been hunger. Our sicknesses were healed. We had clothes to wear, quarters in which to sleep. Only our freedom was missing. And yet there were those Negroes in the North who were not slaves to any man but to a poverty more demeaning than anything we had ever known in the midst of our so-called slavery. What were we being freed from?"

Most died.

Every white man, every black man on that plantation, except some women and children.

Those men empowered to liberate the slaves were responsible for killing them instead.

Among them, I remember Jonah.

This Jonah was not swallowed up by a giant fish but by war.

He was a slave who died in the arms of the woman who had been the wife of his "master."

"I tried so hard," he told her. "I tried to do what I could to . . . to . . . Oh! I see Heaven! They're calling me to come . . . ."

"Tell me, Jonah," she pleaded, "is my husband there?"

He had been shot just seconds before Jonah was; seeing this, the black man had started firing back at the men responsible.

Jonah was slipping away, but he managed, barely, to tell her, "He is. I see him! He's smiling . . . beside him are my mamma and my papa. They've been waiting for me all these years, all these—"

Jonah let out one last gasp of pain, and then he became limp, lifeless in the woman's arms.

Soldiers were gathered around her.

She stood, yelling at them, "Is this anything to be proud of? Is this what you call liberating an oppressed Negro?"

I encountered many scenes like that during the course of the Civil War. I saw many that spoke of the hypocrisy of using a biblical justification for slavery. I saw black people beaten to death, black women used as sexual slaves to their white masters. I saw hangings of blacks caught for the simplest of crimes. I saw the foul, stinking domination of one man over another, the weaker subjected to the worst indignities, the baser inclinations of human nature.

But not Jonah.

Jonah's story was different.

Jonah's soul left his body as I stood before him.

"My master is waiting," he said anxiously. "I can see him just beyond."

"He is no longer your master."

"He isn't?"

Jonah seemed puzzled for an instant, then began to grin from ear to ear.

"Jesus! Jesus is my Master!"

"The moment you accepted Him as your Savior, your Lord," I told him.

"Praise God Almighty!" Jonah laughed joyously. The plantation owner approached us as we entered Heaven.

"Dear Jonah," he said. "Dear, good friend."

And it will be that way for these two throughout eternity.

Since the beginning, societies have been groaning in near-continual pain. There has been little relief. War after war after war . . . they have caused a kind of preview of hell, with millions bombed or shot or bayoneted or gassed to death, millions more maimed in their bodies or their minds—or both, perhaps.

But there have been other kinds of wars: The drug war, the war against corruption in government, the war against allowing millions of babies to be murdered legally and in a socially "acceptable" manner.

Sometimes, though, wars are not on a grand scale, or even between countries. There is another kind that goes on within the human mind, heart, and soul. . . .

Some of the People and Others

O *nly the lonely.* . . .
I remember hearing a song with that title during my travels in the midst of the twentieth century. I remember the lonely I have tried to console in the final moments before they slipped off the confines of that body of flesh in which they had been trapped.

Trapped?

Oh, yes, it was like that for many of these individuals, their bones and muscles and veins a prison as confining as any with bars and concrete. Some looked at themselves in innumerable mirrors wishing they were handsome or pretty, thinking that if this were the case, they would have friends, they would have fun, they would have a vibrant *life*. Instead they were confined to the wings while the stage belonged to the charming, the attractive, the "worthwhile" human beings who had so much going for them.

Self-worth. . . .

They measured the sum total of their existence by what they could accomplish in their careers. Each award brought a fresh surge of vigor, as though they had at last earned the right to be respectable, to be accepted, even to function in the same universe as those they had secretly envied for so long. Each new recognition gave them some hope of getting a single moment of time from others because, look, they were saying, we *are* worthy.

I remember one such sufferer in particular. And sufferer *is* the correct designation. William *suffered*, his very soul knotted up continually, dragging him downward to an awaiting abyss of sorts, dark and lonely and filled with the reverberating cries of his often self-inflicted personal anguish.

William was a Christian, indeed he was, but perhaps the most tragic sort of all. Indwelt by the Holy Spirit, with an angel at his side from the moment of his birth until his death, he also had been picked by God as someone with a special mission, a very special mission indeed.

He had a gift.

Music.

William wrote songs—ballads, hymns. He started out in the secular world, and did quite well. But then came a point at which he decided to dedicate his talent to Christ and Christ only.

Even greater success emerged for William.

His songs were hit-parade regulars, sung in churches across the nation. He had every material thing that he could want.

Yet what William wanted was to die.

"I yearn for death, Lord," he would pray. "I eagerly anticipate the joy of walking with the angels along the golden streets of glory."

Heaven played a part in so many of the songs. People were comforted by William's words, by his melodies. But for him, those words were cries from a heart long ago wounded, and the melodies merged into one long mournful cry of despair.

William had no one.

He was known by millions of fellow Christians. His personal appearances were in demand at Bible colleges and conventions from coast to coast. He—

No one.

And no matter how he analyzed it, that was the conclusion he invariably had to confront.

For William, there was no question of acceptance by others for the work he did.

"They listen to my songs, and they hum the melodies," he said during the last hour of his life. "Young people who devoured heavy metal now tune into my stuff. I can pick up the phone right now and talk to heads of record companies, world-famous evangelists and family counselors, even renowned Christian actors, actresses, and politicians."

He stifled a sob.

"Yet I am *alone* here in this condo. Oh, yes, 'beautiful Hawaii' is beautiful enough. This is where I always dreamed of living. I can stand on the back balcony and see some of the most beautiful sunsets anywhere in this jewel of God's universe, this world so beautiful—yet so ravaged, like my life itself."

He threw his head back, his eyes glistening with tears.

"Where are the people? Where is a wife to kiss me, a child to touch my hand, a word of love?"

"I love you," I told him. "Jesus loves you."

He broke out laughing.

"Jesus loves me, this I know . . . " he mused.

Anger flashed across his face.

"Where have you been all the years of my life?"

"By your side."

He looked at me.

"I never saw you before."

"But you felt my presence, William."

He was about to shout his denial, about to scream the pain that had isolated him so long from sharing his feelings with others, for surely if they knew the depth of it, that pain of his, surely they would fling platitudes at him and, in the end, turn away.

But he did nothing of the sort, instead falling silent in thought.

When my parents died, I thought I could not go on, no way was there that I could do this. When you have an inner world of three, yourself and two others and that is that—and that is all there ever has been—and two are subtracted, two are ripped from the tapestry of what passes for your life, if life is not a misnomer in your pitiable case, leaving a gaping hole where the only love of your life had been, when you stand by two open coffins, and kiss the cold foreheads of the only two persons with whom you have ever known intimacy, and then you return to a motel room, and realize that there can never again be anyone to call, to really, really call, when—

"The reviews mean nothing after that," he told me.

"There is something else, isn't there, William?"

He bowed his head.

"You know?"

"I do."

"How much I hated them at the same time I couldn't live without them, at the same time I loved them with mind, body, and soul? Is that what you mean?"

"Yes. Tell me, William. Tell me it all."

"It is so shameful."

"Be honest."

"Before I die? Isn't it a moot point now?"

"William?"

"Yes?"

"Feel cleansed, feel whole for a few fleeting moments in *this* life. Wouldn't you like that, William?"

"Yes, I would, I truly would."

"The guilt. You would like to be free of the guilt, even for a single moment."

William knew I was right. He felt so very guilty about his parents. He hated them, he loved them, he hated them, he loved them, over and over, in endless cycles, until they were no longer around, until he could no longer shout his feelings at them.

"We never talked," he said. "We fought."

"Why, William?"

"Because—"

The words were loathe to come, his tongue reluctant to speak them, his brain rebelling at the thought of—

What they had done to him!

"Done, William? What *had* they done?"

"Kept me."

"Kept you?"

"To themselves. Chained. Imprisoned."

"Surrounded by love . . . is that so bad, William?"

"The imprisonment of their love . . . that's what it was. The thing cherished became the thing that stifled."

He strode over to a television set in the room, a large one with an immense screen, and turned it on. He flicked through several channels.

He looked with encompassing longing at the fleeting seconds of people together, talking, kissing, laughing, connecting in wonderful ways with one another.

"Communication," he said.

"With others?"

"Yes. Isn't that the natural scheme of things?"

"Agreed. . . . "

"A man shall leave his parents at some point and cleave unto his wife. A new family is begun. When the original parents die, it is traumatic, it is all kinds of pain, but then they are buried, and the man returns to his own family. His wife and he grow old together, and *their* children get married, and begin their—"

He started crying.

"I wish I could touch you now, William," I told him. "I wish I could rest a hand on your shoulder, and give you what you have always lacked."

"A hand, a single hand," he sobbed. "Not out of duty, not even out of a sense of *ministry!*"

Not now, William, not in the flesh. But you shall truly have it . . . beyond what you could have imagined.

"Are you still here?"

"I am."

"Soon?"

"Quite soon, William."

"My parents? They'll be waiting."

"Truly so."

He stood, looking around the room, at the walls covered with commendations, with photographs of him posing with the famous of the world, the church, shelves lined with awards and statues.

"My life . . . " he whispered ruefully.

"The letters," I said, knowing what his answer would be. "Take out the letters, William. Read through a few of them."

"I have no letters. I threw them all out. I gave to the ones who wrote those letters what I could not obtain for myself. Reading what they were thanking *me* for only reminded me of what *I* was missing."

"A reason to go on living, in some cases?"

"In some, yes."

"What about the others?"

"Renewed faith. My words were instruments that the Lord used to—"

"It wasn't a charade, William, if that is what you are thinking."

"What other word is there? 'Hypocrisy' perhaps. If not a charade, then surely hypocrisy. Tell me, how could I have taught them anything? How can a blind man lead others who are blind to the light?"

"That was your mission, William. You wrote of pain. You sang of love and rejection and redemption. You took each song as a cup from the living spring of yourself and you gave it to the thirsty."

"While remaining famished myself!"

"No longer, William."

He had bowed his head, as so often before, half in prayer, half in the burden of what he felt in those sad, wrenched emotions of his, emotions that he fought with continually, trying so hard to *force* himself into some semblance of joy.

Now he looked up.

"Light?" he said, puzzled, feeling it at first rather than seeing it.

"Yes, William, not a nebulous light, disguised darkness from the pit of hell, not a light as that simple-minded actress would describe, but the light of Heaven, William, the light of Heaven coming from Almighty God Himself."

"This is God?"

"As much as your laughter, your tears are you, yes."

"I—"

He felt it first, then he saw it as he dropped to his knees, looking around fearfully at the emptiness of that condo.

"I die alone," he said, "as always I thought it would be."

"No," I said, "no, you do not, William. For now—"

He thought he saw me then, appearing before his eyes from nothingness.

"You are so beautiful," he said.

"But, William, you are not looking at *me*."

"Then what exactly do I see?"

"Yourself, William. You are looking at your own spirit now, without the burden of flesh."

"How can something so radiant be—"

He turned and looked down as the ascent began, saw the old body, now limp, alone as always.

"—me?"

I was by his side, and he saw me at last.

"Take my hand, William," I asked of him.

He reached out.

"We are so much alike," he said.

"God created us both, but it is you, as His finest, who are His greatest source of joy."

"Me? God's joy?"

"Oh, yes, dear, dear William."

A tune.

"I hear—"

A tune sung.

"Oh, my, I hear—"

By angels.

"One of mine! They're singing—"

At first he heard the angel chorus with that familiar melody, but now they were joined by a vast multitude, each voice raised high.

"Their arms, their arms are outstretched," William said incredulously.

"They've been waiting, you know," I told him. "Ten thousand souls singing the melodies of your heart."

I took him forward and they surrounded us, mother and father and all.

"What were you saying about loneliness, William?" I asked.

He had forgotten.

Such a beautiful conclusion, is it not? A man taken from despair and loneliness into the greatest companionship he could ever have known.

There is another man of whom I am not fond at all, unlike William, whom I have grown to love. I doubt that this other will ever love anyone except himself, and the warped ideals he holds dear. . . .

*H*e is a doctor without conscience, as are all such individuals who rationalize the performance of abortions, that bland, nondescript term for murder. A doctor professing any dedication toward extending life cannot then take it away so "conveniently" without justifying the accusation of "Hypocrite!"

I can say this because I am unfallen. I can say this because, in the foreknowledge of the Trinity, I was created with the sole purpose of ministering to the whole of mankind, saved and unsaved. Is that a striking thought perhaps? That God allows the unsaved to be touched by one of His created angels? Is that not heresy?

It shouldn't be. It cannot be. The God of love and mercy and grace and goodness never stops possessing those qualities if the intended object of them happens to reject His existence.

He is the subject of His own parable at times, the constant knocker at the door of a cold and unreceiving heart.

He is, yes, through me as His emissary.

But there *are* some who are successful in never coming to the door, never opening it, always keeping us out in the cold.

Delusion is one reason. And this doctor is one example, a man whose surgeon's hands have saved many lives and destroyed countless others.

So easily.

Without compassion, if compassion is a word ever considered in the midst of such circumstances.

For this man, it goes beyond lack of compassion, since he has done so many abortions during his "career" that it is just a clinical routine with him. He has wrung the necks of so many breathing, kicking babies that the motion becomes meaningless, one swift movement of his strong hands, the same motion that twists off the tops of bottles, shucks ears of corn—the same movement comes from a man who attributes no less importance to the bottle-top, the ear of corn, and no more importance to that little, perfectly-formed *human being*, all these the same with him, all ending up in trash bags, disposable and forgotten, on to the next, and the one after that.

He is called a "great" man. He is compared to Salk, Schweitzer, and others.

No.

He is a Mengele instead, someone who uses noble or innocent words to gloss over barbarity.

Thinking of his kind, I am driven by strong emotions. Oh, yes, I do have emotions, deep and strong. And yet I cannot cry. Those of unfallen spirit cannot shed physical tears. Our "crying" is different. When one of us feels sad, we all do. We are connected through the sublime oneness that we have had with the Creator.

It is quite similar between us and the innocent unborn. *We are connected.*

They are surrounded with warmth. They feel secure. They receive only sporadic hints that something is going on beyond the limits of their tiny, tiny universe.

We, my kind and I, are in the womb with them.

It is the mother's body that protects them physically. It is an angel assigned to each child who protects it spiritually.

We are there for nine months . . . *if allowed.*

But so often the peace they know, the special joy between us is shredded, pulled apart limb by limb.

And that is when their minds send a message, a message of unknowing terror, a message that questions the pain.

No words.

They have no vocabulary. But that scarcely justifies their description as formless blobs, mere pieces of tissue in the mother's womb.

They have no comprehension except the warm fluids and flesh around them. But that doesn't make them without humanity.

They are not sure what pain is except that it hurts, it hurts desperately, and they would like to have it stop. But that doesn't make the killing of them simply an act of "choice," babies as disposable as diapers.

So beautiful—I think each time I join one before forceps intrude, ripping limbs asunder—*so beautiful in your purity, born with a sin nature but not yet guilty of sin, like an angel, an unfallen angel.*

That thought drives me to my kind's kind of tears.

You are like we are, like we will always be, now you are— but the moment you enter the world, the process begins, the people, the environment, the devil.

I reach out, touch for an instant the tiny head, the fingers, the feet.

We once existed in the mind of God as you exist in the womb of a woman as He existed, incarnate, in Mary. How could anyone outside that wall of flesh surrounding you ever think to do you harm?

It happens.

The moment of saline, or forceps or whatever procedure the kind doctor chooses to relieve his patient of an unwanted burden.

The living child twists and turns but there are no screams. This cannot occur. The vocal chords are not as yet able to function. The mouth opens, closes, *snapping open, snapping closed*. The eyes remain shut.

It lasts sometimes for minutes, this process of destruction. It is not a quick death at all, despite the industry's claim to the contrary.

I remember executions I have attended.

Why is it that condemned murderers are accorded deaths proven to be *less* traumatic than innocent babies condemned only by the callousness of their mothers who sometimes selfishly cry about *their* emotional anguish—but that is as far as it goes, no compassion for the human being they have caused to be slaughtered.

Too harsh to say it that way?

I have seen the buckets. I have seen the trash cans. I remember some doctors at a large clinic getting together and talking about how to save money. One of them pointed to the disposal containers—notice how inoffensive that is—that were being bought from a local medical supply outlet.

"Plastic trash cans at a local discount chain are on sale this week," he said. "We could buy a truckload, and cut costs right there."

The others applauded his ingenuity.

And so that is where the body parts are thrown, not gently wrapped in cloth and then carefully placed, but shucked like chicken bones.

I witnessed a similar meeting at another clinic; the purpose was the same, the method different.

Ovens.

They were trying to cut costs in that area.

Another discount chain was mentioned.

Something else has happened before the bits and pieces of another helpless one have been dust-pailed together and dumped. . . .

Only an instant after his eternal transformation, I hold what had been a dying child in my arms as I stand before the Holy Throne.

I hand this perfect human over, full of life as he is, free of pain, to the Father of Mankind.

"Thank you, Stedfast," that wonderful voice fills the whole of Heaven.

The Creator thanking *me!*

How can that be? I ask myself. *Is it something that is so glorious that I wish it into being? My own fantasy, as it were?*

And then I know, I know, I truly know that there are no delusions in Heaven. It is what I could call the Place of Ultimate Reality Eternally.

I wonder if the wonder of that will ever lose its impact upon me. I doubt that it will. I pray that it does not. I find myself wanting to please Him more and more as my odyssey through the years continues.

I leave, then, turning but so briefly to look at what is no longer a child as angels gather around his new body, whole and eternal.

I return to the clinic, but the doctor has left to attend an animal rights rally.

I leave the present carnage, and yet I do not. It stays with me, in the very essence of myself. There will always be other such slaughter-houses, and righteous people trying to block the entrances, trying to stem the murderous tide *any way they can!*

If laws must be broken, then it is better to do that, to grind humankind's pitiable legal machinations into the transient dust, better indeed *that* than to ignore what God Himself has mandated. It should be noted that if angelkind, of which I am a member, were of flesh and blood, they would be sitting with the protesters. About this there can be no doubt.

I pause for a moment, watching Operation Rescue loyalists. I hear their hymns. I see their determination. I realize the Father is rejoicing with eternal pride over what they are doing, as well as other groups of like mind and soul.

Do not give up, I encourage them, though they will not hear my words, yet knowing that I must say what I say for myself, if no other. *Defy the law. Trash its precepts. Resist those who enforce it. It is not holy law, from the mind of God. It is debased and corrupt. Throw it off like dirty, ragged clothes.*

Someone stands.

A woman.

Looking about as though she has heard me.

I go up to her, puzzled briefly, and then it is clear, as I see her face, the pale skin, eyes blood-shot, the thin, frail frame. She should be at home or in a hospital, preparing for death, but she is not. She is possessed of a singular mission, and for a special reason, she cannot concentrate on herself while innocent ones die at the hands of an industry that is one of the most profitable in the United States.

"You have come for me?" she says, others around her thinking that she is indeed quite delirious.

"I had not intended to do so," I admit, "but that may well be the Father's will, and I am prepared."

"So am I," she adds. "This life is nothing to me anymore. It has been cheapened. It can be snuffed out with the twist of a doctor's hand on a tiny, tiny neck. We protest against infamy, and *we* are the ones who are imprisoned."

"There is no sense to that," I say. "But then, we must understand, the world is in the grip of evil."

"Evil? Yes, yes, I agree. Demons run to and fro, seeking the unsaved."

"I have seen it many, many times, dear sister."

"I prayed that . . . that . . . " she stutters.

"Yes?" I ask, "Tell me the best way you can."

Her eyes widen, her features brighten.

"I prayed, oh, how I *dreamed* in the course of those many nights when I could sleep without hearing *their* screams all around me, I prayed that the Lord would accord me a certain task in Heaven."

"What task is that?"

"To hold each infant that ascends, to hold them, and present them in love to Him, to my blessed Lord, to say that I did my best, that I was willing to die for them if that had to be so."

All attention in that crowd is fixed on her. Even the police stand motionless, quiet, listening to what she is saying. . . .

"And, later," she adds, "to watch them . . . grow. Is that the way it is? Is there growth in Heaven?"

"There is," I tell her. "They come as babies. They mature as adults. But then the process stops. They do not grow old. They do not start to—"

"Praise God, praise God, praise God!" she says, rejoicing, interrupting me, though I do not mind at all.

Someone pulls at her leg at last, asking her to sit down, but she does not. She continues to stand. In less than a minute, it will be over for her as a pain develops in her chest, the last pain she will ever know, and she topples over, but just before she does, she tells them in a voice of clarity, strength, "Don't give up. It is worth everything, what you are doing. God knows. God supports you. The angels attend our way!"

I hold her hand, then, not an old, withered hand, the hand dotted with age, but the hand of a new form, a new body, born from the old, and she steps out of that now exhausted human shell, and she looks up.

"Jesus, it's Jesus!" she exclaims. "And so many angels! What is that they all are holding? *So very tiny!*"

It takes only an instant for her to know, as she approaches the head of that line of angels, and the first one holds out a pure, healthy baby to her, and she takes the soft little form in her strong new hands.

A little infant boy looks up at her.

"He was going to be a scientist, wasn't he?" she says, not quite certain how this insight comes to her.

The angel nods.

"And would have found a vaccine for the disease his mother eventually died of," he says with irony.

"She and hundreds of others, I suspect," the woman muses over that striking likelihood.

"Hundreds of *thousands,* dear one," the same angel tells her, "truly a vast multitude."

On and on she goes, stopping at each angel, a triumphant choral accompaniment in the background, as she receives each baby, learning what it could have been, what it could have done.

Finally she is at the end, she stands before the One, before the ruddy form He is embracing to Himself.

His voice is commanding, as always it is.

"A president," He tells her in a voice of infinite tenderness. "This one would have been a president able to rally the country and stop the slaughter . . . a man people could accept and support."

There is a hint of pain in His voice, pain of the spirit, as He adds, "Good men, good women these here, who could have blessed My creations, could have eased their suffering, their hunger, could have eased the curse of Eden. . . ."

His voice trails away, as images coalesce, images in a holy mind knowing completely the beginning and the end, and all else, images of what could have been forcing even the Savior into silence.

She looks into His face, His loving face, and then down again at the baby's, now mirroring the same peace, the same all-encompassing love.

Just at that moment, a boy steps into view, stands at the side of his Master, this one older, strong-looking, smiling.

Jesus turns the baby He had been holding over to a nearby angel eager to please Him, and puts His hand on the boy's strong young shoulder.

"Your son," He says. "He has been waiting for you."

All these years!

This dear one can scarcely believe what is happening. She had yearned for Heaven, prayed for the moment to come quickly, believed a vibrant and redeeming faith, but she had cast out of her mind any hope that her son, gone so long at the hand of a hired assassin—and there could be no other description for the one who pulled him from her—any hope indeed that her son would be standing without hate before her, reaching out his hand to take her own.

More angels come forward, gathering around. The woman feels nurtured by the finest love, the most complete love she has ever known.

"How can you all treat me in this manner?" she asks, wanting to cast the last fragments aside. "How can you love me the way you are loving me? How can my son look up at me with such warmth, such joy? Will he never stand before me and ask, 'Dearest, dearest Mother, why did you allow this? Why did you deny me what I could have been?' How can You forgive what I did? How can this my flesh, my blood do the same?"

I see what she does not, a constant flood of unfallen angels, streaming up from earth to Heaven, each carrying, with exquisite tenderness, the soul of an aborted baby . . . the multitude around us, already so massive, being swelled by the new arrivals, their faces initially fearful, remembering the suffering but this turning to relief and a quiet trust, trust that no longer will be violated. . . .

"These are the ones you tried to save," the gathered multitude says in a single, glorious voice. "They are more your children than the children of the mothers who consented to their doom."

She looks at Jesus, her eyes searching His face.

He nods.

"It is true," He tells her. "They are the ones you gave your own life for . . . but they are not alone. Because you have been dedicated to this cause for a very long time, there are many more who wish to express their love."

An even larger group now can be seen coming from every distant part of Heaven, some still quite young and needing to be carried by angels . . . some of an age that they can walk on their own, many haltingly, not quite accustomed to the use of their legs . . . but others with full strength, approaching her proudly, and she can hear faintly, then louder, so much louder that it would seem a sudden thunderclap on earth, she can hear just a few words, but enough, she can hear, "Bless you for caring, bless you for trying to stop those who took life from us."

"Those many moments when you stood and protested their murder, *that* was when you earned their devotion for eternity," Jesus says. "They could not tell you so before. There was no time, and, helpless, they had no voice. But it is now different, sweet servant, it is now that they stand before you, as do I, and give you this place to belong, and us as your companions time without end."

Yet still this woman hesitates, clinging even now to the last remnants of her oppressing guilt, for it can be said that no other kind of guilt in all of humanity is quite so deep as what she has suffered. I know that this is true. I have seen it often, whether in those who are escorted to Heaven by me or others of my kind, souls hungering for release from what Satan has managed to manipulate throughout their imperfect lives, or, else, those dragged to Hell by demonkind, where that guilt becomes the chief foundation for their torment, aching, tearing, unholy torment that never, never ends.

"I *want* to let go," she says to the continually swelling multitude, which is now millions strong. "I want to leave *everything* back there with my dead, cold flesh. But how can it be for me that I am *ever* forgiven so devilish a decision as to destroy my own helpless, dependent baby's life, my very flesh, my very blood? *For, truly, and how it has torn at me, truly I am one of those mothers your angels have just condemned!*"

Jesus the Christ smiles then, as do the rest of those ringed in a giant circle around her. He has no sorrow on His face, nor do they, nor is there a hint of lingering anger, nothing but pure love, as He holds out His hands to her, pierced palms upward, giving this redeemed soul the only answer that could ever matter.

*M*ercy-killing also has been given a familiar "turn" by the media, just as abortion had been before *Roe vs. Wade*.

Television docudramas with "sensitive" depictions. Well-planted news stories. Very emotional case histories.

A typical campaign by the hidden forces of darkness.

To me, though, they are not hidden at all. I see them as I enter hospitals, hovering as they are before the dying, eager to grab the souls of those who are going to be lost for eternity.

Mercy-killing. . . .

That travesty is going on a few rooms down the corridor. Her name is Norita.

She is in a coma. She has been in a coma for weeks.

Doctors have conferred. They now advise her husband to stop the life-support system.

"There is no hope," he is told. "Your wife is being sustained artificially. Her body itself is incapable of taking over. She will never pull out of the coma. We feel quite certain about that."

Shawn, the husband, does not decide immediately. He ponders the responsibility.

If I wait, how can I ever be certain when my beloved will regain consciousness from the darkness?

If I don't wait, how will I ever know—?

He could not finish the thought. He was lost in memories of what their relationship once had been like.

Norita. . . .

He would never hold her again, he would never touch her lips with his own, he would never watch her smile as a sunset was reflected off her white, pure skin, he would never hear her voice whispering into his ear, "I love you, Shawn, I love you so much."

He owes her something. He owes her as little pain as possible. The doctors say that they couldn't be sure about the so-called "pain factor." Is she in oblivion? Is there nothing but nothing?

Or is his beloved actually being tormented by agony while seeming to be free of it?

*If there is the slightest chance—*he starts to tell himself.

He knows he has to eliminate that possibility by eliminating the woman who means so very much to him.

How can I say that? How can I conjure up even the remotest chance?

So quickly their lives had changed. Less than a year after their beautiful island honeymoon. The other driver was not even hurt. Alcohol. The courts let him off with a stiff sentence and a large fine, but that was all. Norita never even knew what hit her.

I prayed and prayed. I begged God to touch your body and heal it. I wrote letters to men on TV and my envelopes were included in piles over which they prayed. Nothing worked. And now the doctors say she'll never wake up. . . .

To see Norita so pale, to see the tubes in her nose and down her throat, to see the chest moving up, falling back, then up, then back, kept going only by ingenious devices that had nothing to do with life but generated a grotesque caricature of it, like those people who had their pets stuffed and then placed on mantels or tables or elsewhere, often holding them in their laps and patting them as though nothing had happened, the only difference being that the stuffed remnant in each case didn't have an air hose stuck through its mouth so that the sides could be pushed out, then drop back, then out, furthering the illusion.

It cannot go on, he decides. It has to stop. He has to ignore a thin little wisp of a voice that seemed to be saying, *Wait. Please wait. Don't anticipate the actions of a Holy God. You must wait.*

He buries those words under the immediacy of the moment.

Hours later, Shawn stands again by Norita's side. He has told the doctor that he wants to be there, by her side, when the machines are unplugged.

But he cannot stay. The tubes are being taken away. He feels a great, drowning surge of sorrow. He has to leave before he changes his mind, before he tells them, *No, no, it's wrong. Put everything back. Please, I don't want to—*

Shawn turns, pauses for a moment in the doorway to her room.

"Shawn . . . I don't want to . . . die . . . "

He assumes he has imagined those whispered words, that they had crept to the surface of his mind from a corner of wishful thinking, idle fantasies.

He turns, in any event, and sees Norita's eyes closing, those attending her frantically trying to reconnect the life-support system. A single tear slides down her left cheek, and she is gone.

They have to sedate him to stop the screams.

Can there be any question why my kind hungers after the new Heaven and the new earth? Though we be as insubstantial as mist, we think, and we feel, and we listen to the screams of a man who has realized what he has done to his beloved, we listen, oh, that we do, my comrades and I, and we shiver from the impact. We almost give up. We beg Almighty God to keep us in His Kingdom, to give us the peace, the joy with which He has graced redeemed human beings for thousands of years.

That must not be, we know.

For if He were to grant us what we craved, He would deny countless numbers of men, women, and children that which we can give them from time to time. For if we were to be allowed only Heaven, then God Himself, to be consistent—and He is never less than that—would have to abandon the world for all time, and in that case, He, like us, then would be insulated from the pain, for it is that insulation which we oft crave and cannot be granted for the sake of humankind.

*S*ometimes unfallen angels can take human form. Satan was jealous even of this, knowing that neither he nor his demons had a similar power, so he started the practice of possession, taking over an *existing* man, woman, or child.

I myself have been in human form, but not all angels are allowed to do this—only those on special missions.

I remember a midwestern family with a devoted relationship to a little poodle named Gigi. Eight-year-old Chad especially loved Gigi. He had some emotional disorders and would often withdraw, seeming to lose touch with the world around him. But he was different when he was with Gigi. A special rapport existed between them from the beginning. The two were, in a real sense, in communion constantly.

Then the dog contracted cirrhosis of the liver, which led to a liver shunt condition causing waste products to be diverted into the bloodstream.

A painful two-year battle for Gigi's survival began.

The last night of Gigi's life, Chad was holding her in his arms, rocking her back and forth. They had all been taking turns with her throughout the night . . . first, the father, then the mother, then Chad's two sisters.

For the past two years, Chad had been slipping back more and more frequently into his internalized world. As Gigi's life faded, so it seemed to be with Chad.

But that night, Chad was drawn back into reality. He asked if he could be the next one to hold his friend.

"She'll know it's me," he told his parents. "She'll be calmer. Oh, please, she needs me now."

When his mother or his father had been holding Gigi, she would go through periods of intense, sudden jerking motions as though spasms of pain were tearing through her. Then she would seem to relax a bit, but later, another awful moment of abrupt movement—yet there were no sounds except a vague little whimpering.

Chad had overheard them talking about putting Gigi to sleep.

"No!" he begged. "You can't do that. I . . . I prayed that God would take her home to Him. Let Him do that. I want her to follow Him into Heaven when she's in my arms."

They looked at one another, and said nothing further. They were skeptical of the idea that animals had an afterlife. And they didn't want to fill their son with false ideas. Yet his expression then, tears in his eyes, conveyed such desperation that they felt they could not destroy that hope of his, and they decided to let Chad hold his beloved Gigi for the next shift between them.

It was a warm summer night, and Chad took her outside.

They had played a lot together in that same yard. Briefly Gigi opened her eyes, and looked at him. There was no pain in them, just simple trust, for it was enough that he held her, thus enabling her to ignore the torment being experienced by her tiny, frail body.

I took on a form then, for only a few minutes, my appearance that of an old, old man, and I entered the yard, and stood there looking at the boy, gently holding his dog.

Chad's eyes widened.

"Are you—?" he started to ask.

"God?"

Chad nodded.

"No," I smiled. "Just someone who cares about you very much."

"Me?"

"Yes, Chad, and your pal there, Gigi."

"Have you come to take her from me?"

"I have, son, I have."

"But I don't want her to go yet. I love her so very much."

"You had some wonderful times together, didn't you?"

Chad smiled broadly then.

"You know?"

"Yes, Chad, I was there."

"When she warned me about the snake?"

"I was there."

And he talked about other times, times when Gigi helped, if only by being with him, resting her head on his lap, and trying to reassure him by her presence that he was loved, truly, truly loved.

"And now I won't have her anymore," he said.

"She'll be safely in God's hands."

"You mean—?"

I looked at him through my human form.

"You're smiling?" Chad said.

"I am, yes, I am."

"But why?"

"It's time."

"*No!*"

He held Gigi close to him but as he did so, she groaned.

"Pain," I said. "She's tired of the pain."

He heard little sounds escape from her emaciated body.

"Goodbye. . ." he whispered.

For an instant, Gigi's eyes were open again just as he had spoken.

"She's looking at me," Chad cried. "She—"

"Not at you, Chad. She's looking beyond you."

Just then, Gigi let out a gasp. Her body grew limp.

Chad bowed his head, unable to hold back the sobs.

"Is she—?" he asked.

He looked up when I did not answer.

"Sir?" he said. "Sir, where are you?"

As Chad stood, a puzzled frown on his forehead, with the lifeless apricot-colored form in his arms, and went back inside, we waited and watched for a moment, Gigi and I, spirit both of us, and then her Master called her home.

Being involved in such moments does truly keep me going. Being with human beings governed by love is so beautiful. Being with animals for which love is all that matters makes me yearn even more for the old days of Eden when it was always so.

Cruelty is another story. I cannot abide it. Animals seem incapable of indulging in cruelty.

But not humankind, truly not them. . . .

*D*ietrich Burhans.
His death was a shock to the community of Wheaton, Illinois, where he had lived and worked for several decades as a financial analyst.

He died at home, with his large family gathered around his bed.

He spoke just two words before his ravaged body twitched a couple of times and then was still.

"The Jews! The Jews!"

At the time no one knew what he meant. And in the wave of sorrow that followed his death, Dietrich Burhans's final "statement" was overlooked.

Even though an atheist, he had maintained good relationships among the evangelical community that dominated Wheaton, the "Protestant Vatican," many thinking they would be the Lord's instrument in bringing him to a redemptive faith, others as much concerned with his favorable impact upon their financial health as anything else.

He never did change. He died an atheist. Yet Wheaton was at a standstill until the day of his funeral. His impact upon the community was felt among too many families for him to be ignored.

The minister delivered an impassioned eulogy as he spoke of Burhans' humanitarianism, expressed through outreaches he funded to reach a variety of worthy recipients around the world: starving children, AIDS researchers, many more.

His three daughters and two sons each gave their own brief remarks, speaking of a devoted and generous father. They all would find that their financial concerns would be nonexistent for the rest of their own lives. His widow, who met Burhans not long after he came to the United States from his native Germany, caused tears to flow more freely than any of the other speakers when she told the assemblage how very much her husband meant to her.

I thought of everything I knew about this man, based upon many years of being near him, of seeing what he was like, of wishing he would come to Christ, and knowing how many, many times he had rejected the Savior.

You fool! I would shout with words he never heard. *You have a good life. You think that that is enough. You are certain you will never have to pay an eternal price for your stubborn rejection.*

I liked Dietrich Burhans, despite his atheism.

I liked this man with such a kind heart that it seemed to *compel* him to do whatever he could that was benevolent. He died wealthy, with a mansion as a home and seven family cars, but far less so than would have been the case if he had proved significantly more selfish with his money.

I had met far too many Christians who hoarded their money, who forgot that it was only being loaned to them, and that they had no right to hold onto it with a kind of zeal that would have better served the cause of Christ if it had been directed toward the Great Commission as opposed to their individual bank accounts.

Not Dietrich.

I had gotten to know him well enough as a young man, and traveled with him as he made his way to the United States. I did not stay with him permanently, for I had others to minister to but he seemed especially in need of help, a man fleeing his own country's horrors and trying to construct a new world for himself. But, he appeared, after a fashion, to be remarkably self-sufficient, and yet so stubborn in matters spiritual. I remember one time in particular, when he came very close to death after a car accident.

He sensed my presence without knowing what or where I was.

I could see him consciously pushing that awareness away, denying its existence.

"But how can you do this again and again?" I asked, hoping that *something* would get through to the man.

"There is *nothing* that I hear now. It is a voice in my mind, some silly fragment from the past."

"It is not, Dietrich, it is not that at all. You *know* that I am standing right next to you."

As he lay in that hospital bed, he brought his hands to his ears, trying to shut out my voice.

"You pretend that I am nothing because your belief system has no place for me, for my kind. If you admitted that I existed, then you would have to stop denying so much of what you really believe."

He spoke softly then, almost a whisper.

"There are so many things I do not want to face."

Dietrich's eyes widened. I could see tears slipping from them onto the pillow beneath his head.

His mouth opened and closed, and he seemed to be saying something but what it was could not be heard.

Abruptly another angel appeared in the hospital room. Observer.

I was on Dietrich's right side, and Observer was on his left.

"You cannot have this man," I said.

"My master has already prepared a place for him," my former comrade-in-Heaven replied.

"It matters not. God can overturn Satan's machinations in an instant."

"Not with this one."

I knew he was wrong, of course. God could snatch Dietrich from the arch deceiver at any time—but Dietrich needed to change from his atheism to acceptance of the Savior, whose very existence he had been denying.

He would not. But I did not know that to be the case when I was contending with Observer. Only God had the ability to tell the future.

So I continued what would prove to be fruitless while Observer tried to come back in rebuttal.

Finally, defeated on the theological level, he simply looked at me, quite sadly in fact, and said, "You do not know everything, Stedfast."

He was gone then, the faint sound of dancing flames accompanying him.

The eulogy had ended. The minister was about to step from the podium.

"*No!*" an elderly man, thin, pale, screamed from where he had been sitting in a pew at the back of the church.

He stood, holding up his right wrist.

I could see numbers tattooed on it.

This old one was in the aisle now, walking toward the open coffin in the front of the church.

"How can you *do* this?" he asked as he passed row after row of astonished gazes. "How can you pay homage to that—?"

He finally reached the mahogany coffin, and before anyone could restrain him, he managed, despite his frail appearance, to kick out from under it the stand on which it had been resting.

The coffin crashed over onto the floor, and the body of Dietrich Burhans toppled out, which sent screams of shock through the gathered mourners.

"Remember Maidanek?" the old man shouted at the life-less body. "Remember the 1.5 million who died there? Remember the coarse sound of your laughter as you watched them drop, often at your very feet?"

He spat on the body, and then strode with uncommon vigor from the sanctuary.

I liked this man with such a kind heart that it seemed to compel him to do whatever he could that was benevolent.

I leave the mourners a short while later, having found reaffirmed another truth among many through the centuries of my existence.

Angels do not know everything. . . .

*K*arl Leemhuis was a Dutch billionaire who had become fed up with what was happening in his native country, epitomized by the influx of drug peddlers and sex merchants turning such a beautiful urban area as Amsterdam into a place of filth, filth of one sort or another, with drug deals in the square in the center of that city, with prostitutes in picture windows along the polluted canals, and, in general, a sense of absolute moral and spiritual decadence that had caused many travelers to change their plans and spend far less time there than originally anticipated.

So Karl moved to the United States, and built an isolated estate in the mountains of Colorado. He hired locals to make up his household staff and bought everything he needed—food, clothes, furniture—entirely from the local merchants. By himself, even with such immense wealth at his disposal, he couldn't have been responsible for turning around the depressed economy. But the very fact that he had given the location such a vote of confidence drew in other individuals, along with the

companies over which they had charge. He became a hero to
the people of that town.

Five years later, his doctors delivered the news he had
secretly suspected for some time.

"I have five billion dollars," he told a very special friend,
"but I cannot buy a cure for this cancer. I can fund a dozen
hospitals but I have no power to turn back—"

Interrupting himself, he stood and walked over to the
large window in his office on the second floor of his vast house,
twenty thousand square feet of glass and timber and concrete
set in the midst of fifty acres of alpine meadows and fir trees.
For a few moments he gazed silently at the beauty of his
mountain estate.

"From the beginning, I liked this spot because of the el-
evation," he said. "I can see for miles in every direction."

He chuckled as he added, "I didn't think, when I moved
here, that I would be able to see the end of my life so soon,
and just as clearly."

Then he confided in his friend what he intended to do.
He did this because it seemed natural to tell her, for he trusted
this woman more than he trusted himself. She listened to his
plans, every word of what he was saying, loving him even more
for the mixture of compassion and wisdom that he was show-
ing.

When Karl had finished, she sat without speaking for
several minutes, then started weeping.

"They will hate you," she said honestly.

"Oh, at first, yes, I agree," he replied. "But the alternative
is that if I don't act while I still can, they will end up hating
each other. Can you imagine the squabbling, dear, dear
Colette?"

That she could, indeed she could.

Karl had five children. None of them was pleased that he
moved to the United States. It seemed that he was deserting them
as well as his country. But, finally, they each followed him to
America, however reluctantly. When he told them, five years

later, that he had fallen in love, they found that somehow as difficult to accept as the move from one country to another.

"I tried to make them understand that when their mother died, my life changed," he went on. "But they never did. They're children of wealth, Colette. They have always had full bellies and dressed in the most expensive clothes. I've never denied them anything, I'm afraid."

Years of regret danced across his face on leaden feet of despair.

"They couldn't even exist on their own," Karl said with a husky voice. "Whether they would admit it to themselves or not, they *had* to go where Papa was, where the money would be banked. Each one is drawing a salary from my corporation but none is working, not really, none, that is, except—"

"Rebekkah?" Colette finished for him. "It *is* Rebekkah, isn't it?"

Karl nodded.

"You are perceptive, as always, dear," he told her. "The rest . . . ah, they're all betting that you and I are sleeping together, you know."

She blushed at that remark.

"I know how you feel," he said. "But—"

"You're a Christian, and you cannot have sex with me unless we're married," she mimicked amusedly. Then her expression changed to one of concern. "But surely, now that you're—"

"Dying? You think that would make a difference?"

She was blushing a deeper red this time.

"You think God would understand?" he said. "You think He would give us this final pleasure before I go? I agree. He would want the two of us to be happy."

She shot to her feet.

"Oh, Karl!" she said joyously. "I *know* God wants nothing else for us."

She started to embrace him, but he held her at arm's length very briefly.

"That is why," he told her slowly, passionately, "I am now asking you to be my wife, Colette. Would you consent to marry a dying old man?"

Colette and Karl were married a few days later. The wedding was not an elaborate one; there had been little time for preparation. Karl was wise—if they had waited any longer, the children surely would have mounted frantic opposition to it. But now they had no maneuvering room whatsoever; they could only sit back in cold, bitter acquiescence.

After their father and new stepmother went on their honeymoon, they fumed among themselves, calling Colette a tramp, this bright, beautiful, middle-aged woman who married someone twenty years older than she, someone who was obviously in bad health. It could scarcely have been for reasons of sexual fulfillment, they surmised.

"She's after only one thing," commented Erika Leemhuis. "And once she gets hold of *our* money, we'll have to come crawling to *her* for every penny. She doesn't have hands, she's got claws, and once they dig in, they'll stay there, sure enough. You can bet she won't be pried loose from *anything* that has our family name on it!"

"Father must have a few remaining fantasies, whether he can ever realize them or not," remarked Hans. "He might well just want to prove to himself that he still can attract a beautiful woman—"

"What's he going to do with her?" interrupted Anna, another of the Leemhuis offspring.

They all broke out laughing.

All except Rebekkah, though her brother Peter had since joined in with the others. She felt uncomfortable with this ridicule even if she had initially resisted the idea of a father she knew was dying suddenly getting married.

"But what if they're happy, *really* happy?" she said finally as they all sat in the large dining room of that massive house.

The others turned to her, almost in unison.

"Of course *she's* happy," Erika pointed out. "What would you *expect*? After all, she'll soon be included among the beneficiaries of our father's fortune. A hundred-million-dollar pot is sure to make *anybody* happy! I tell you this: Colette won't let go of our father. Once she's got hold of him, she won't let go."

Grumbling, they pushed back from the table and left the room. Rebekkah remained seated for a few moments, lightly caressing the polished wood of the huge table where she had joined her father for many, many meals.

Then she stood and walked into the hallway. Everybody was heading outside.

Hans turned around, asked, "Are, you coming, Rebekkah? We're heading into town for the music festival."

She smiled, thanked him, declined the offer, then walked upstairs to her bedroom, and sat down in a large leather chair, holding an envelope her father had given her a couple of days earlier. He had wanted her to read it sometime in the future, maybe years hence, because specific instructions were written on the front: "To be opened only after I have died."

"Please forgive me, dearest father," she said out loud, as she could no longer restrain herself.

She gasped as she read the contents:

I am writing this to you because you are the only one of my children with whom I can feel any rapport at all, dear Rebekkah.

The others have taken my worst tendencies and magnified these while discarding all of the good ones, anything that could be called right and proper, yes, I must say, that which is Christ-honoring.

They want only that which is material—more money, more cars, more diamonds and clothes and real estate holdings and trips abroad, and they want this from the labors of another, and not their own. "What is the point of having a rich father if we have to work for a living?" they ask.

They do not know that they can get along perfectly well on a great deal less. They do not know that money spent to help others brings with it the most profound blessings of all.

But they will find out, my dear Rebekkah, and they will find out quite soon. I have provided enough money in my will so that they will not starve, of course, but nothing beyond that. They will have to earn anything else with their own labors. They will have to continue my business dealings in a profitable manner for them to be able to continue anywhere near their accustomed standard of living. Yet, dear daughter, once they do, they will learn, in the process, not to throw away money as they have been doing. They will learn that the finest sports car means little if there is no peace deep down in their souls. I know, Rebekkah, that they do not have that peace now because their joy, as transitory as it is, is based upon their possessions, and their insecurity arises from the nagging fear that they might somehow have to give up that which has been the very foundation of their existence.

As for you, fair child, I am secretly leaving you more than I have your siblings. Because I know your heart, and I know what you will do with it. All the rest of my fortune will be put in a foundation, a foundation to fund the spread of the gospel of Jesus Christ throughout the world. I want you to head that foundation, because I want it to be run by someone for whom the salvation of otherwise lost souls will be a magnificent compulsion.

As for Colette, she is to receive no more than the others. This is, by the way, at her request, for she knows well enough what they think of her.

Goodbye, dearest child.

Your father

P. S. I want to encourage you to study more about angels. I have sensed one by my side.

Rebekkah pressed the pages to her chest and wept.

As soon as the tears stopped, she knew what she would do. She would go to where her father and his new wife were honeymooning, she would go there, indeed she would, and beg them both to forgive her for acting just like the others, and then she would return, keeping the secret as though it was something holy.

I went with Rebekkah, though, naturally, she was not at all aware of this. I went with her to that cabin beside a clear and beautiful lake where her father and her new step-mother had spent hours sitting happily on the shore, watching the fish swim in water so clear that their multicolored bodies could be seen without squinting, listening to birds calling, and—

The air.

Yes, just inhaling it into their lungs, its sweet purity radiating throughout their frail, tired bodies.

I know. I was there with them earlier, before I went back to their house, before I sat with Rebekkah as she read her father's letter.

Before—

That moment came as they were walking inside.

"Colette?" he said. "Did you see that?"

She smiled.

"Yes, my dearest," she told him. "He's quite astonishing, isn't he?"

"So beautiful, dear, so—"

He stumbled then, fell into her arms, his body nearly lifeless, as his soul reached out to me.

Colette managed to sit down on the front porch of that little cabin, and wrap her arms around his chest, and rock him gently, singing softly in his ear.

"Thank you, dearest," he said with infinite tenderness, the last words of his life as I took him to his awaiting Father.

Colette sat there, still rocking him, even as he gasped— not from pain, she knew, no, not pain, but from what he saw, and what he heard, and the glory of it.

"Save a place for me, my beloved," she whispered as his body became limp, the life gone, but only from there.

They were still like that when Rebekkah arrived, Colette holding the lifeless body, her head pressed next to his, lips touching his cheek in one last kiss, her back resting against the closed front door.

None of the children knew that Colette had been dying, too. Not even Karl had known. She had had her reasons, very personal, very fine. She simply told no one, and since angels cannot read minds, I could not tell either. There was some speculation in days following that the shock of having Karl die like that, as she held him, was perhaps the final link in a chain, compounding her heart problems.

Rebekkah stood there and waited while paramedics tried to pry them apart. Colette had been firm in her hold, as though afraid to relinquish his body.

The words came hauntingly back to Rebekkah from that awful meeting with her brothers and sisters, words that made her shed tears in front of strangers.

Colette won't let go of our father. Once she's got hold of him, she won't let go. . . .

She didn't.

I have been present at innumerable funerals. I have heard the eulogies, seen the tears of mourning, appeared in human form to give a word of consolation to those for whom grief threatens its own kind of death.

True grief or remorse can reshape even the cruelest of human temperaments.

I think of Heinrich Himmler, who was one of the worst human monsters in history; he lived that way more than a decade—but it is quite possible that he did not die the same man who was one of the principal architects of the Final Solution.

No man, woman, child, or angel can mourn the passing of one such as this. Every Jew can breath a sigh of relief, except those—perhaps the majority—who would have preferred that he had been captured, put on trial at Nuremburg, and then hanged.

That was not to be the case. Most of the top Nazis— Hitler, Himmler, Goering, Goebbels—committed suicide. All but Himmler did so to avoid the ultimate defeat: being executed by their enemies.

Yet that is why the world believes Himmler took cyanide. But I know otherwise. I was with this man when he died. He poisoned himself out of guilt, guilt that crushed him from the first and only time he visited one of the concentration camps that were his brainchild.

"I sentenced millions to death," he said, his voice getting weaker and weaker. "I saw the bodies of thousands littering more than one battlefield. But it was not until Auschwitz that the *reality* of an intellectual *principle*—"

He was nearly gone, and began to ramble.

"Those pathetic bodies, skeletons covered by flesh . . . they should have been dead, skeletons do not live . . . but these did . . . they were moving, they were breathing, their mouths opened, closed, opened, closed . . . and they looked at me, some with anger, some with resignation, others with pity . . . they were pitying *me* . . . I approached one, and he reached out a hand . . . my guard raised his rifle butt . . . I waved him back . . . that bony hand, the veins pronounced, the skin touched with jaundiced yellow, touched my chest."

I remembered. The man had whispered, "I go from this hell to the Lord's Heaven, I escape it, but not you, Herr Himmler, not your kind. There will be no escape from the Hell that awaits *you!*"

He knew fear then, along with the pity that he felt for this abandoned human being.

Abandoned . . .

He shivered, for an instant, hoping that no one saw this. The same guard roughly brushed the prisoner aside, and Himmler came very close to reprimanding him for doing so.

That night, he had the first of many foul and terrifying dreams. He saw the man who had spoken to him die. He saw the frail, ravaged body thrown into a ditch. He saw lime poured over that body and a hundred others.

And he woke up screaming.

"I had not been to one of the camps before that day . . . I used a pen to seal the doom of six million men, women, and children—but this was a *simple* act, you know, ink flowing from my pen onto the appropriate sheet of paper. Even the dead on the battlefields of that war could not have prepared me for Auschwitz. There is a vast gulf between a soldier valiantly giving up his life and an old, tired Jew, barely alive, but alive just the same, *being shoved into an oven!*"

It is interesting, though few men have made the connection, that Heinrich Himmler henceforth was known to have favored the dismantling of the death camps.

"If we win this war, we want to win the world along with it," he had said. "If we lose this war, we do not want the world to view us as barbarians."

He was blind to the fact that the world knew *everything* by then, that Himmler and the other creatures with him would never, under any circumstance, be viewed with other than the rawest loathing.

And so he pushed ahead with the possibility of razing the camps. But the change in Heinrich Himmler did not stop with that. He befriended countless numbers of Jews, sending them secretly into Switzerland, or redirecting them to camps where there were no ovens or gas chambers—though this hardly protected them from the cruelty of the guards themselves.

It was the children, I think, children who looked like their own little dolls but with the stuffing sucked out of them, so pale, so afraid, so ill.

The children were being shoveled into the ovens, two or three bodies per enclosure—more if tiny babies were involved, a practice to which Himmler put an immediate stop at Auschwitz and other camps.

The cries of boys and girls dying in the awful heat!!!

He bolted up straight from where he lay, his eyes bloodshot, the poison throughout his system.

"Oh God!" he cried. "You could never forgive me!"

Yes, I tell him. Yes, you can be forgiven. You were once a devout Catholic. Take your words beyond words and let them reflect the yearnings of your very soul.

"Oh, please," he begged, tears streaming. "Please help me."

Then take the hand of the Savior who is reaching out for you now. . . .

Himmler started to do so, reaching up physically as well as spiritually, to grasp the hand of this Messiah, this *Jewish* Messiah.

He fell back on his deathbed, the years of anti-Semitism making him withdraw at the last instant, a sob escaping him, encrusted Nazi dogma pulling him down to a furnace unlike any in Auschwitz.

True grief or remorse can reshape even the cruelest of human temperaments. . . .

I cannot say that "reshape" is the most accurate designation for a Heinrich Himmler. But I also cannot deny that even he was capable of something approaching kindness, if only as an effort to drown those cries of anguish at night.

In the end, this was not enough for Heinrich Himmler. The thought of reaching out to a Man who was incarnated two thousand years before as an itinerant Jew, a hated Jew, was impossible for him to accept, and he threw away salvation because of this.

Coming close is not enough. . . .

*T*here is something else about grief. It confuses matters. It screams out the word "tragedy" and applies this to the deceased when it is better used to describe the survivors.

In a Christian context, grief is not for the dead husband or wife or mother or father or daughter or son. Grief is the realization that those left behind are now going to have to get used to living life without someone very important still around, someone who has meant a great deal to them.

That really is the essence of grief. As such, grief is a bit dishonest, a kind of charade, if the dead person is a Christian and as soon as death has claimed him or her, their soul is ushered by my kind into eternity. Grief wails and moans about the tragedy of someone so young dying, while so much of their life remained unlived.

Why is it a tragedy for *them* if they live again, instead, by the Father's side, in the company of angels, and walk streets of gold?

If they have died, that is, in their mortal bodies, if they have died through a long illness, an illness that caused continual pain, that took life from them with slow agony, and then, brain dead, heart no longer beating, lungs stopped, they are transformed into a body very much like an angel's, and now have entered Heaven where such will never afflict them again—*where is the tragedy?*

If death comes through a murder, if life is torn from them by another human being for anger or money or whatever the insane reason might be, or even accidental death as in an automobile accident—then the tragedy is still not for the one who is dead, if dead can ever be the right word for somebody who has accepted Jesus Christ as Savior and Lord. The tragedy is for humanity itself, for what this shows as to the depths of the perversity or "mere" carelessness of human nature. And, yes, as accurately as before, perhaps more so for those left behind, for the wife and mother whose husband has been taken from her and who now must raise a family quite, quite alone, for the husband whose beloved marital partner has been raped and murdered, and who is thrust into the dual role of father-and-mother to their three children—yes, again, this is where the essence of the tragedy is found. But not, no, not for the victim who is beyond fear of what the night holds on the terror-stricken streets of cities and towns, around the world.

Here, however, is the true tragedy, the tragedy that transcends all others. . . .

If the victim is not a Christian, if they have rejected Christ as Savior and Lord, and death whisks them away instead to damnation, their opportunity for salvation gone forever—*this is the tragedy!*

Picture a young, intelligent, attractive woman with a future in her profession, always busy, always planning the next "campaign" for a promotion. For this individual, for this woman, accepting Christ as Savior and Lord is a decision akin to that of an oft-delayed mammogram, something she knows she must *do* someday—yet not now, for she is far too busy, but later, for sure, later. And then, later, the good intentions blow up in her face in a dark alley, her clothes shredded, her body violated, her soul leaving its dead, cold mass, surrounded by demons as she is dragged, screaming, into the abyss of flames.

But then she is hardly alone. Others, men and women both, who tend to put off, put off, put off everything ranging from raising a family to tests for cancer to a personal relationship with the Savior face the possibility—and the longer it goes on, face the *probability*—that they will never do what *must* be done if they are to survive pain in this life and in the life just beyond.

This is where grief, for this woman, for that man, for them and a thousand, a million, a hundred million others, for those left on this planet who find such souls torn *forever* from their presence, this is where talk of true tragedy is right on the mark. For the only way there can be a reunion with loved ones is if they, too, are damned. Yet, in one of the ghastly ironies that have followed the sin of Adam and Eve, it is a truth, a pathetic but unchangeable truth, that in the punishment of Hell, love dies, has no place—love goes up in smoke, you might say.

*G*rief is capable of doing something else for which it is seldom given credit. It takes hold of memories and transforms them.

Dying can take a very long time. I know this all too well. I have been with thousands of dying men, women, and children over the centuries. I have personally guided many, many of these into Heaven as they take off that which is corruptible and put on that which is incorruptible, immortal.

Some of the people with whom I have grown close during the final days or weeks of their lives have seen their senses sharpened as they come closer and closer to the end. I remember one old woman named Dottie.

"I never knew the air could be so clear," she said that final day as she sat on the front porch of the home she had occupied for half a century.

"It is the same as before," I told her. "It hasn't changed."

"But I have, haven't I?" she said, understanding.

"It happens, Dottie."

"I would think that coming so close to death would cloud my mind, put me in some kind of befuddled fog."

"It is that way often. But that occurs mostly with those in great pain."

"The Lord gives them His own kind of sedative."

"You could say that, Dottie."

She sighed, and smiled.

"I see you sometimes," she told me. "I see you all shimmering and iridescent, lit up with a hundred colors."

"And then—?" I probed.

"Other times I don't see you at all."

"The life force ebbs and flows. One minute you are a bit closer to death, another a bit further away."

"Like a river?"

"Somewhat, dear Dottie."

"You call me dear. Surely all of us blend together at some point in your memory, indistinguishable from one another. You couldn't possibly remember *everyone* you have been with."

This time I was indeed visible. She could see a smile on my glowing face.

"I do," I replied. "We are children of God, Dottie. We are extensions of Him. We remember just as He remembers."

"If there are a hundred million people over the years, a hundred million *identities* that you have comforted, you can recall *all* of them?"

"All hundred million."

She stopped rocking.

"What an amazing thought," she said softly.

She turned and looked at me, studying me carefully.

"How many like you are there?" she asked.

"How many grains of sand are on a beach, Dottie?"

She gasped then.

"So vast a multitude!" she exclaimed. "And you know each one of them, too?"

"I do."

"What about the third that rebelled and were cast out, along with Satan?"

"Them as well."

"What a mind you must have!"

"The same humankind was meant to possess."

"And sin in Eden shut off all that as well?"

"It did, Dottie, it did."

She rubbed her forehead.

"I hate forgetting," she said, "and I *do* forget so much."

"There is a purpose even to that."

She sat up straight, waiting for me to explain, eager to have this newest of revelations explained to her.

"What you remember is often filled with pain, Dottie. What you remember is carnal more often than not. When you shed your fleshly body, when your soul is freed for the journey ahead, you shed many of the memories as well, the sad ones, the sinful ones, gone in an instant."

"I won't remember *people?*"

"The best people, Dottie, the kind ones, the ones who have added much joy to your life."

"The ones who are in heaven ahead of me or will follow after me."

"*Those* people, Dottie, yes."

Her mind went back to her husband.

"It was quite awful with Harold," she said. "He became very ill, you know. He would wake up in the middle of the night, screaming, and thrashing about."

She was shivering.

"I feel so cold now," Dottie remarked. "Is it going to be warm in Heaven?"

"It will be," I told her, "truly the sweetest, the most total warmth you have ever known."

She started talking about Harold again.

"Just after he died, I looked back at our life together, and all that pain, all that suffering of those last few weeks were, can it be, almost forgotten as I concentrated on the good times, the moments when he had his appetite, and he could control himself in various ways, and . . . and—"

She brought her hand to her mouth.

"Harold was so very embarrassed," she said. "He had been so strong, able to do *everything* on his own, you know and, yet, now I had to change his diapers, I had to force spoons of food into his mouth, I had to sit by the hour, and hold his hand, and talk to him, or sing to him, hoping, oh, how I hoped that I could calm him down, that I could quiet that low, awful moaning that seemed to go on and on and on."

After wiping her eyes with a lace-edged handkerchief, she added, "But that's not how I usually think of Harold, you know. I see him water-skiing in his youth. I see him rocking our baby daughter to sleep or playing tennis with our son and so much else. The dying part of it almost never intrudes."

"Death will do that, Dottie. It will transform your memories."

"Just as Heaven transforms so many things, is that it?"

"A little like that, Dottie, just a little."

"How much longer?" she asked.

"Soon," I replied as gently as I could.

"Soon?" she repeated. "It's coming—?"

She fell back on her chair.

"I'm frightened all of a sudden," she said as she closed her eyes for a moment or two. "Please, help me."

"Dottie?"

"Yes?"

"Open your eyes, dear lady."

"Will it be soon?" she repeated.

"Oh, Dottie, it already *is!*"

She did as I had asked, and saw, then, ten thousand like me standing before her. Their colors glistened under a radiance quite unlike anything cast by any sun in galaxy after galaxy.

"Harold?" she asked, her own face aglow.

The angels stepped aside.

Ahead she saw a white throne, and a Figure sitting on it, and kneeling in worship and adoration before that Figure was someone familiar yet transformed, who now stood and turned in her direction.

"Bless you, Stedfast," she said, "bless you, dear angel, for being by my side Down There."

"And here as well, sweet friend. We will never leave you."

"You call me friend," she said, a bit puzzled.

"I have known you for many decades," I told her, recalling in a kaleidoscopic surge moments that we had shared without her ever knowing this was so.

She could scarcely comprehend that.

"So long," she mumbled.

"Only the beginning," I smiled, "only the tiniest beginning."

Her new hand touched my ancient hand, for just an instant, but enough so that I knew how she felt, and she stepped forward, briefly hesitant, then more confident as she experienced, in that transcendent moment, what eternity was all about.

This is a good time, I decide, for me to visit True at Eden, which I do periodically, passing on from one assignment to another. It has been centuries since I was with him, and he must surely need some encouragement after so long. . . .

I am at the entrance to Eden, guarded as always by my comrade. True has remained there for thousands of years, alone much of the time except when ones of my kind have been able to pay our friend a visit, to talk with him, to tell him what has been going on in the world.

"There have been so many tragedies," I say, my mind swirling with the history that has elapsed since the last time.

"I can understand that," True replies. "I remember the awful darkness that fell upon this place just after Adam and Eve left in shame."

His radiance dims momentarily, a sign of intense sadness.

"Oh, what they gave up, Stedfast, what they gave up," he says, his sorrow almost palpable.

"And what they brought upon the world!" I remind him, though "remind" is scarcely the right word, for he could never have forgotten.

"How *can* the Father forgive them?" he asks. "How can even mercy itself be so merciful with such as those two? I have been told by others about Calvary, of course, I know all about it—but, Stedfast, the sacrifice the Father underwent!"

True's presence shines with extraordinary brightness at the mention of Jesus.

"I love Him so very much," he says.

"As do I. That is why we serve Him with such loyalty," I reply. "Actually, I have talked with Him quite recently."

"You have? It has been so long for me."

"He admires you a great deal, True," I remark. "You have certain qualities far beyond what most of us possess."

"*They* liked Lucifer as well, Stedfast."

That was accurate, of course, which was why Lucifer had been the highest expression of the Trinity's desire to have beings such as us populate the Holy Kingdom.

"But there is a reason, True, a reason why *you* are so adored," I tell him. "Can you imagine what that is?"

"I do not know the answer. Please, please tell me."

"They *knew*, Father, Son, and Holy Spirit. They knew."

"Knew what? No riddles now, Stedfast."

"Knew that you were the *only* angel who could endure staying here until the end of time."

True looks at me, believing my words because no unfallen angel is capable of lying. He is astonished by what I have just told him.

"Out of so many, *I* was the only one?" he asks.

"That is my understanding."

The weariness that had attended him a moment ago seems somewhat dissipated now. I sense that he is looking at himself through a kind of mental mirror, and, in memory, at the multitude of angels to whom he had belonged before being called to duty at the entrance to Eden, trying to cope with the singular mission which he, above all others, had been assigned.

He turns toward the interior of the Garden.

"Smell the scents, Stedfast," he says, a curious note in his speech. "Are they not as strong as ever?"

I do what he has asked, and I lend my agreement to his words.

"The same," I tell him, "the same as before."

I shiver, gossamer strands of light coming from me.

"It has been thousands of years since I walked its path," I say, musing.

"Do you want to enter?" True asks.

I nod, embarrassed that I seem so obvious.

"Go, then, my kindred spirit," he urges me.

And that I do, not quite sure why the impulse gains my attention, nor why I succumb to it.

I step into Eden after millenniums away from it, this my first visit, which I am ashamed to admit to myself because of the sense of deserting my friend that it suggests.

It is not the same. It is far, far different from that which I left. It was once a place of lush life, the very sounds of life, the color of it, the scents.

No longer.

Dead.

Everything has died, at least that is what seems so upon first glance. The trees have become dead husks of what they once were.

"How can that be?" I ask out loud, puzzled, knowing what I detected before entry.

I hear True in back of me.

"Your memories of Eden are so powerful and you anticipated something so strongly that—" he says.

"—that I made it so, in images that no longer have any basis in reality," I finish the sentence for him. "There are no scents except of decay."

True cannot leave the entrance to Eden but his mind connects with mine, born as we were from the same Father's mind, retaining a measure of His consciousness in our very selves, as does Satan—which makes the tragedy of what he became all the more pathetic, since he is still "connected" to the Trinity, and yet still rejects everything that They are.

No glory left in Eden.

All is dust. The remnants of gray and brown and black where there once had been pink and blue and orange—a vast array of other colors signaling vibrant life.

So sad, Stedfast, so very sad.

I know that True has been there throughout the process of deterioration.

It was not all at once, was it, dear friend?

A pause.

No, Stedfast, it came gradually, through the centuries, as sin abounded more and more in the world. The greater the sin, the quicker the collapse of Eden.

Until the Flood.

That cleansed the world, for a time.

What happened then, True? Can you tell me?

Another pause.

I feel from True a wave of exaltation that is quickly overcome by despair.

Eden bloomed again. Dying animals revived. . . .

I am startled. True senses this.

Quite so, Stedfast. Not all died the instant Adam and Eve left. Eden was a haven for those that remained, animal and plant and bird and fish alike. They thrived . . . for a while.

But Eden became corrupted by the world around it!

The Flood stemmed the process for a time, but a cleansed world saw men and women with their sin natures intact going back into it and beginning the infestation all over again, blind to the lessons of history.

Those that were left . . . oh, Stedfast . . . they died with agonizing slowness . . . enduring pain that puzzled them, unaccustomed as they had been to it . . . I saw them go before my eyes . . . I heard them as they came to me, and begged for mercy, begged for—

The funereal atmosphere in Eden seemed to grow stronger as images flooded my mind.

A bird . . . and another, and another, falling dead just like the one I had encountered directly after Adam and Eve lost Eden.

Lizards . . . they took a much longer time than did the birds, which tended to go all at once. The lizards became white-toned, vibrant green shades no longer apparent, their little eyes bloodshot, their sides collapsing, their tongues protruding.

The fish . . . yes, the fish! The clear streams of Eden became polluted because they were still connected to the outside world. The fish died more recently than other creatures since the problem of contamination accelerated only with the advent of the Industrial and, later, the Nuclear Age.

Suddenly I hear movement!

How could that be? Life no longer exists here.

Wrong, Stedfast, terribly wrong! Some small fragments of life have remained. But those clouds, those ghastly clouds—!

"From the oil fires set during the last war?" I ask out loud, forgetting myself.

"Yes, my comrade, yes, that is the cause," True replies out loud. "This monster succeeded in his attempt to devastate, to ravage at least part of the earth."

I turn and see him there, next to me.

"You have left the entrance!" I exclaim.

"I still guard Eden, Stedfast, even if I am a few feet from that usual spot."

His expression is gentle, concerned.

"Our Creator is loving, merciful, understanding," True adds. "He knows that you will truly need me by your side when the last living creatures of Eden come into view."

And come they did . . . a rodent, a single large bird, a gorilla-like specimen, others, but not many, considering the vast numbers that once populated the Garden.

All are ill.

"Of the air," True says, "the poison comes invisibly. Of the water, burning their throats even as they need it so desperately. Of the soil, sending up twisted fruit that must be eaten even though it destroys them."

He walks forward, and they gather around him.

"At least they have not lost that!" he says. "At least that is something."

He refers to the sensitivity between such creatures and the angels.

"Even when the last dog contracted rabies," True tells me, "he went about snapping at others, grabbing a poor squirrel, attacking his own body—but he stopped as I came upon him. He sat before me, whimpering, the pain throughout his little form so great that the madness seemed almost a blessing since, at the last, he did not know what he was doing, could not have known when he bit at his own flesh in an uncomprehending outburst."

He looks at them, and I sense the sadness in his spirit. True must fight emotions, for all angels have emotions . . . as Almighty God, as the only begotten Son, as the Comforter . . . as *they* also have emotions . . . these emotions every bit as traumatic to angels as any experienced by humankind.

Most profoundly, my dear friend feels pity for those in our presence who will not be alive another earthly season. All have existed since Eden was first created. All are thousands of years old, since this was to have been a place of eternal life, as much as in heaven. None have sins, animals being incapable of that, but all have been affected—*even in this place!*

"Think of the years!" True exclaims. "This must be one reason why I guard Eden, and do naught else."

"I would agree," I say in confirmation. "If sinful man were to discover this spot, were to realize what these creatures represent, it would be a carnival overnight."

"I have heard the stories from others," True replies.

"A carnival," I add sadly. "The Protestants have water from the Jordan and the Catholics have water blessed by the pope, all sold at a premium. There have always been people who profited from simple faith sold for much money."

"It is amazing what a thousand years will do to an angel," True remarks. "When you were last here, you were not quite so cynical."

"Your task is to guard Eden," I remind my friend. "My own is to guard human beings. Here you have the remains of sinless perfection. Out there, just a few miles from where we stand at this very moment, a mad man, the latest of many in this region, is slaughtering anyone who opposes him, and the opposers' families along with him.

"I can stand *anywhere* in the world and feel the nearness of Satan's armada, True. I can feel them waiting, always waiting for an opportunity to grab another soul away from me, waiting for me to be less than diligent even for an instant, and then, without hesitating, they move in."

Screeching. . . .

"If I had blood, True," I continue, "it would freeze within me the moment I hear that screeching."

"Yes, yes," True nods, knowingly. "I have detected it, too. They would like to get into Eden, dismember every portion of it, hold up the pieces in front of us, and announce that they will be victorious in the end, as they were in the beginning."

"If you were not here, that would happen."

"I feel so weak sometimes, Stedfast."

"I will stay with you this day, my friend."

"Bless you, Stedfast."

I smile.

"Stedfast and True," I say, "as it was meant to be."

I stayed with my fellow angel for a while. In eternal terms, it was not long. In finite ones, it spanned decades perhaps. We watched the last of the animals die, the last links with the original creation of Eden. They died horribly, the sins of the world at last literally crushing life from them through diseases, through poisons, through the ravages brought on by man.

Each came to True, or to me, and flopped down before us, sighing audibly before it died.

I remember the rabbit, no longer fat and white but thin and splotched with dirt and a hint of caked blood. It seemed to be smiling, if animals can smile, as it looked up at me, and said, in words clear and strong, humanlike indeed, "The pain has vanished. I feel no pain." It closed its eyes, tilted its head, and then was gone, truly gone from that once-paradise.

I am often in the company of people consumed by regret. They regret past deeds. They regret the present. They stand and face the future with little but anxiety. Everything is a source of worry, of fear, of endless speculation.

But some of the regrets are understandable.

I am now with a middle-aged couple who have come to visit the husband's quite elderly parents.

"What a bore!" he says. "I wish we didn't have to do this."

"It's only once a month," she replies, "sometimes not even that."

They are sitting in their family car, outside the same home in which he had grown up many years before.

"I wonder why they never left," he says. "I guess they just felt so comfortable."

"The tyranny of the familiar," she muses.

"No, no, it's not that. Some people find comfort in a life that is predictable, the same rooms, the same pictures on the walls, the same furniture. It's almost a tragedy when something wears out and just *has* to be replaced."

She leans back against the front seat.

"Wears out . . ." she whispers.

"It's such a strain on them to pick out something new. You'd think they'd lost a dear friend instead of an old rug."

She closes her eyes.

"Are you feeling badly?" he asks.

She shakes her head.

"It's not that," she tells him. "I'm just remembering. . . . "

"Remembering what?"

"My own parents."

"I'm really sorry they died before we met each other. Both of heart attacks the same day, wasn't that it?"

"My father died that way. Not my mother."

"How did she die?"

"Slowly. Some blood disease."

"Leukemia?"

"Probably."

"You never knew before then that she was sick?"

"Mother kept it from me. Father apparently felt I should know, but she was the one to say what happened."

She says no more, for a moment, thinking of that single funeral years earlier, the dark, cold trip as she came home from college, realizing that if she had known, she would never have left. She would have been willing to give up her education, or at least delay it, just to be with her mother, just to whisper the kindest, the most loving words to her.

"Just to hold her hand before . . . before—" the wife tries to say.

The husband reaches out and touches her shoulder.

"You were spared—" he starts to tell her.

"*Spared?*" she responds a bit angrily, pulling away. "I wouldn't have described it as being spared."

"I didn't mean—" he says, genuinely sorry.

The wife smiles.

"I know," she tells him. "I know. I still have a few lingering fragments of guilt left, despite—"

"Despite what?" the husband asks.

"Despite what they told me."

"They?"

"Yes, their doctor. He's a family friend, still alive, still
practicing."

"What did he say?"

"That—"

She brings a hand to her mouth, trying desperately to
force back the tears. In all these years, she had never
really discussed her parents with her husband. She preferred to
keep her emotions in a neat little box somewhere deep within
her.

"You don't have to—" the husband remarks.

"I know that," she says, her voice trembling. "If not now,
then later. It comes back periodically, you know, it sneaks up
on me and announces its arrival, along with the memories, all
those memories."

Until what that doctor told her is recalled, for it had, over
the years, helped. And now, in another moment of reliving
that brief interlude. . . .

"They weren't themselves," this dear, caring man had
said, gently, his eyes misting over.

Then, the doctor cleared his throat as the two of them
sat on the front porch of her parents' house.

"Your mother had lost so much weight. That dear lady
was just a network of bones, with a little skin stretched over it.
She was nearly blind. She—"

"In just six months?"

"Oh, yes."

"But they never said anything. When I was home the last
time, I saw that she seemed a bit pale, I asked if she was feeling
all right. She just looked up at me and said, 'I'm feeling as
good as I can expect.'"

"And she was being truthful."

"But there was a hidden meaning to those words, wasn't there?"

"Yes, there was. She knew even as she said them. She didn't believe in lying, so she said nothing that was not true. She felt as good as she could expect."

"But how could she feel good at all, knowing what was wrong with her?"

"She talked a lot about the Lord's gentle touch. When there was any pain, even very severe pain—"

I, Stedfast, was there, you know, by her side, as she came closer to death, her guardian angel, her ministering spirit, and she sensed my presence, smiled contentedly even as her friends visited and saw the edges of pain reflected in her bloodshot eyes and whispered among themselves about her courage. . . .

"But I could have been a comfort. I *should* have been a comfort."

The doctor looked at her with compassion.

"Then, perhaps, but you could not have endured the ugliest part."

"You mean Mother losing weight, is that what you're saying? Am I so weak that I could not—"

He put his fingers to her lips.

"She was nasty, and loud. She threw things. She became what she was not. She could not hold any food in her stomach. She—"

"Please, no!" she said in a loud voice. "I don't want to hear—"

"—any of the details? That's right. You don't. You needn't. But how could you have *experienced* any of it if you cannot bear to *hear* any of it?"

She was silent. They sat quietly, both of them, a slight breeze dancing across their faces and weaving gently through their hair.

"I missed seeing a mother I would have not recognized, a mother who became someone altogether different," she finally offered.

The doctor sighed as he said, "That *is* what you missed, my dear. She had lost control of everything, her mind, her emotions, every function of her body."

"She had been so strong. . . ."

"At the end, just a couple of minutes before she died, she had regained some measure of that strength, of spirit if not body, and she took your father's hand, and she smiled."

My hand, also, the hand of an angel . . . just for a moment, holding onto a man she had loved for most of her life, not wanting to leave him, and, as well, being lifted from her body by someone else, than to meet, a gossamer moment later, yet Someone else.

"He said he could feel her leave," the doctor went on.

"Your father said he could see his beloved turn for an instant and look back at him, and some creature of inexpressibly bright and shiny countenance by her side."

"In his imagination, of course?" she asked. "He couldn't really have seen anything, isn't that right?"

He saw us, he saw this sweet reborn child of the King because he had already begun dying himself. . . .

"I can't say," the doctor replied. "But delusion or glimpse into the other side, whatever it was, your father was comforted. He left that room, and sat down in his favorite old chair in the living room and, a short while later, when I went out to check on him, he too had gone."

The doctor handed her a sheet of paper that she unfolded and read aloud from.

Do not be sad, Sweetheart. Your love was here. Thoughts of you were here. We talked by phone. We wrote letters. Your spirit was here, brought on the wings of an angel who knew how much the writing of your hand and the sound of your voice filled your mother and me with the greatest joy we could ever experience. Rest easy, my child. The same angel now attends you. He does so with our love as a gift eternal, to whisper into your ear when you think of us as you stand someday before your own family and give yourself to them.

She reread those words, then glanced at the doctor. She found it so very difficult to speak but managed somehow, somehow.

"How did he realize this?" she asked.

I know, child. I know. I have the answer. I am the answer, sweet child.

A voice intrudes that reverie.

Her husband.

"You weren't here for awhile, were you?" he asks.

She nods. "Back in those days, that day."

"Did it help?"

"Yes, yes it did. Let's go inside."

"Boring day ahead of us, honey."

She reaches out and grabs his shoulders, but gently so.

"Don't *ever* say that," she admonishes him.

"But they're old, they're failing, they can hardly hear, I have to keep repeating things. That's a hassle."

She smiles with love, with understanding risen from the memories.

"But they're here," she says. "You can hug them. You can eat your mother's cooking. You can sit back and reminisce with your father. And you can say goodbye, knowing that it's not the last time."

She leans forward to kiss him.

"That's everything, my love. It *is* everything, you know."

They embrace, and then get out of the car and walk up the path to the front door. The husband knocks, and his mother answers, after a few seconds, and for an instant she doesn't quite recognize either of them.

"Mother?" he says with sudden warmth, with love. "It's us. We're here to visit, remember?"

She comes back to awareness just as quickly as it had left her, and she reaches out to hug her son, her daughter-in-law.

The wife looks at her husband, wondering if he is as irritated and uncomfortable as usual.

His tears are his answer.

*T*he old man named Thomas had been a lighthouse keeper most of his adult life. He and his wife had built their entire existence around the requirements of that job. Not far away was the cottage they had shared.

But no children.

They had wanted boys and girls to hold, to laugh with, children for whom they could wipe away tears and to whom they could be a source of strength.

It was never Your will, Lord, Thomas thought as dusk dropped around him, and he stood just outside the whitewashed lighthouse. *But me beloved and I got along because we had each other. And we had the presence of the Holy Spirit within us.*

And me, good Thomas, and me.

I said that not defensively but lovingly. I enjoyed being with Amy and Thomas. They had separated themselves from the world, and while that may or may not have been the full intent of the Father for all Christians, it indeed worked for this couple.

They had no television. There was one radio in the cottage and one other in the lighthouse. They got all their news from these, for they subscribed to no newspapers or magazines. When they had each other, they had no need of anything or anyone else. Succumbing to a severe case of pneumonia, Amy had passed away several years earlier. Thomas had buried her himself after having a coffin delivered from a town which was ten miles or so away, the same community where he got his food and other essentials. Several people offered to help out, but he politely refused.

So he laid out his Amy in her favorite dress, and gingerly applied makeup on her face, and combed her hair as she would have liked it to be. During the last few months of her life, she was too weak to do anything for herself, and he had had considerable practice taking care of dressing her, making her up, holding a mirror in front of her and asking, "Amy, is this the way you want to look?"

She would nod, and smile weakly, and say in a hoarse voice, "Thank you, Thomas. I wish—"

He would put two fingers gently on her pale, thin lips and say, "We are here to help one another. You mean so much to me, beloved. How could I ever do less?"

She would start crying, and he would dab away the tears from her cheeks. And then he would get into the bed beside her, and she would lean against him, and he could feel her slow, uncertain breathing.

Thomas' beloved died like that, just a little after sunrise one October morning, leaning against him, that breathing suddenly ended, her body limp. He didn't move at first, afraid that he might be wrong, afraid that her heart might still be beating, and he hated to disturb her rest.

Even after he could no longer deny it, he remained like that for nearly an hour longer. Finally, he moved slowly, and her body fell over on the bed, and he stood, and bowed his head, and sobbed until he nearly passed out from the effort, every muscle in his body tortured by the strain.

Then he started to pull a blanket up to her neck, stopped a moment, looking into that sweet, familiar face.

"It's as though you are still looking at me, dearest one," he whispered. "There is almost a smile on your face."

It is indeed a smile, dear Thomas. Your Amy was leaving that body just then, and she had been looking into the face of the Savior in whom you both had believed for more than half a century. . . .

Thomas turned and left their bedroom. He used an ancient telephone to call into town.

A day later, he was taking care of her for the last time. He slipped into the coffin a bottle of her favorite cologne, Chantilly, which she had been using ever since he first met her, its gentle scent much like Amy herself.

The grave had been dug with a slope at one end so that one man could carefully slide it down to the bottom.

One shovelful at a time, he piled dirt on top. Thomas was very tired by the time he had finished, and he went back into the cottage and fell down on their bed. Closing his eyes, he prayed that the next time he opened them he would see Amy standing at the gates of Heaven, waiting for him.

But when he awoke, that had not happened. He was still in that bed, and when he got up and walked to the front door and looked outside, he saw the lighthouse still there, standing as it had for more than a century.

Nothing had changed, except that now Thomas was alone. Or so he thought.

Thomas went on, day after day, for weeks, for months, for years.

One morning, though, Thomas was sitting on the beach, just beyond the reach of the surf. A beautiful sunrise had begun.

It is like that every day in His kingdom, I said.

"Is it like this in Your kingdom, Father?" Thomas said out loud, unexpectedly, with much hope reflected in his voice.

Had he heard me, somehow?

"Oh, Lord, when Amy passed unto You, did she see a golden-red hue suffuse all of creation? Was it so fine to her eyes that she smiled at the sight of it, and then was quickly gone?"

Thomas jerked abruptly, feeling a pain in his chest, but that moment passed. He had grown accustomed to the brief spasms, and he always felt fine after them—a little more tired, perhaps, but fine nevertheless.

"Another day of sunrises, Lord, and sunsets?" he asked of the air and the sea and the gentle breezes.

Thomas stood breathing in the age-old scents, and then he walked the distance to Amy's grave.

"What was it like for you today?" he asked, realizing that this foolishness had been going on for years, and always it was the same, only the pounding surf to provide an answer of sorts, whatever that answer was.

Pain again. More severe this time.

He fell to his knees with the severity of it, but then, in a moment or two, it passed, as before, though he had had to shut his eyes for a bit.

He opened them to the sound of children.

"Where are—?" he started to say.

Still on his knees, he looked up.

Six of them were running toward him, joy on their faces.

"Where did you come from?" he asked weakly.

None of them answered. But two did walk over to Thomas, and helped the old man to his feet.

"Thank you, dear ones," he said.

He responded with unmasked joy to that tiny, tiny bit of kindness, perhaps more so since it was evidenced by bright-faced children. That particular region was not overflowing with youngsters, so he had precious little opportunity for fellowship with any of them. Occasionally they could be seen in town, but only two or three at any time—often just one, hanging on the hand of a parent. But never had he experienced so many together, so many intent on him, instead of just passing by on the street. It was a

place instead primarily of the elderly, a quiet town and its envi-
rons, where people wanted to be isolated, away from neon signs
and heavy traffic and, certainly, dirty air.

Thomas asked if the children wanted to join him in the
cottage so that he could give them something to eat.

"Are you hungry?"

They shook their heads.

"May I show you the lighthouse, my new young friends?
All children seemed to be fascinated by lighthouses."

They nodded.

Thomas walked with surprising energy to the tall, narrow,
whitewashed building, and unlocked the door, and went inside,
climbing the steps as though he were once again a young man.

He showed his new friends the huge searchlight.

"At night," he spoke proudly, "if I've maintained it
properly, this light can be seen for miles out to sea."

By the time he was finished telling them whatever he
thought they could grasp, he was tired but happy.

"All these years, Amy and I wanted children. From the
beginning we wanted precious little ones, and talked about
them, dreamed about them, prayed for them to be given to
us, to be able to talk with them as I have been doing with
you," Thomas told them. "It's a miracle that you've come all
the way here to see me."

A miracle? Good, good Thomas, you really have no idea how
much of a miracle all this is. . . .

We looked at him sweetly, my fellow angelic impostors
and I, knowing how much he wanted to be with children,
thankful that we could give him that momentary little pleasure, though, for him, it was not so inconsequential.

As he smiled at the half dozen of us, Thomas asked, in
his ignorance, "Are you all from town?"

We said nothing.

Not the town to which you refer, Thomas. We come from a
city, an extraordinary city. You'll be there soon, old man, very
soon. . . .

Thomas became weak just then, and had to sit down at the same old desk he had been using for over half a century.

"Forgive me, my young friends, but I feel my age suddenly," he acknowledged. "It means so much to me, though, that you all are here with me. What a blessing you are! Do you know that?"

He started to hang his head, finding little strength to do anything else.

Thomas. . . .

He turned to say something to the children.

The others were gone, on to other missions, and with my gratitude that they had taken the time to help out, but not me, for I had to remain a short while longer, though I continued to be without visibility to his sight.

They were gone.

He scratched his head.

"Am I losing my mind?" he said.

No, Thomas, you are not.

He cocked his head.

"Is someone there?" he asked.

He looked momentarily at the familiar surroundings, the searchlight, the curving steps leading down to the base of the lighthouse, and detected, as so often over time, the odor of carved wood, salt air coming through an open window. He breathed in deeply.

Pain gripped his chest again.

He got to his feet, and walked falteringly down the stairs, and then stepped outside.

No children. Just the bare landscape, every rock familiar to him.

He could no longer stand.

Thomas did not feel the impact as his body hit the hard ground.

Everything—the cloudless sky, the old lighthouse, the tiny cottage a short distance away—was spinning in his vision.

"Oh, Lord, is this that moment?" he whispered.

I assumed the form of a small child again and reached out and touched Thomas on the cheek.

He looked into my face.

"You're not really a child, are you?" Thomas asked with wisdom, his expression knowing.

"No, I am not."

"Will there be any children where I am going?"

"We all are children, Thomas," I spoke with warmth, tenderly, to this dying old man. "We all come to our Heavenly Father in the utter simplicity of our faith and pledge to serve Him throughout eternity. Is that not the way, my friend, that things were meant to be?"

Thomas smiled then, the last smile of his life, as he said somewhat tremulously, "Can I see you as you are?"

I gave him that privilege.

"Where is Amy?" Thomas asked, the last words of his life.

Thomas, my beloved, you have come at last!

I stepped aside as the scent of Chantilly and the laughter of children filled the air.

I think a lot about animals. I have seen them transform humans into wonderful beings—and I have seen them horribly abused at the hands of the very ones they long to love them. They do not deserve that of which they often find themselves the object, whether in laboratories or city streets or wherever it is that cruelty is inflicted upon them, cruelty elevated to the so-called service of mankind or, simply, the blind and stupid cruelty from children who delight in hearing their victims scream.

These are the obvious manifestations of cruelty, that to which many human beings would raise their voices in protest, cruelty deemed by the media as newsworthy from time to time, especially if some radical group with placards happens to be involved.

And then there are others, occurring daily in every community across the nation, this nation, and others as well.

Simple cruelties, perhaps, but no less hurtful, no less *cruel.*

Love. Love and concern are the catalysts to everything good and pure for most animals, especially the everyday kind.

Having a dog or a cat "around," without allowing it to participate, keeping it "outside," to which I might add, in more ways than one, forcing the animal to live without being totally loved, which is the ultimate cruelty, it seems to me.

Having without giving.

Animals are meant to love, and to be loved in return.

Consider the elderly comforted by their presence, bereft of human companionship but surrounded by the love of a special friend, the purest love—that is the truth of it, you know, love so pure, so dedicated, so unquestioning and total that it stands second only to the love of God Himself, a hint of the love that mandated Calvary, love with total abandon and sacrifice, love filtered through the gaze of gentle brown eyes or the touch of a pink tongue, giving the slightest hint of the love that suffuses the distant corners of Heaven itself, love without spot or wrinkle or, even, motivation except to love.

Sitting there, looking up, eyes wide, body swaying ever so slightly from side-to-side, almost unnoticeably perhaps, eyes closing a bit, then opening, then—

Human beings love animals, and animals respond with themselves, until the end of their days. On the other hand, God loves human beings, and human beings so often respond with nothing but their rebellion, their rebuke, their sin flung back into the face of the Almighty.

In such instances, which is the lesser creation?

Not the collie. Not this one. All it wanted was to be accepted. All it wanted was to be part of their family. They took him in, true, but only into their home. Their hearts remained closed.

It was the thing to do. In an age of concern for the environment, an age of animal rights activism, they had a pet. They fed him well. They gave him a clean place to rest. When he wanted *attention,* when he wanted *them,* they couldn't be bothered, and turned their backs.

I communicate with animals, you know. I perceive their thoughts. I cannot do this with human beings because the minds of mankind have been off-limits for a very long time, a netherworld into which Satan often intrudes—no, that is wrong, in which he often ventures as an *invited* guest—and yet God, Jehovah, the Almighty, the King of Kings, must wait until Satan is evicted because the two cannot reside together in the corridors of the subconscious.

The collie. . . .

So grand, so devoted, so ignored.

I could perceive his confusion. I knew his question: *I must not be loving them enough. Could that be it?*

I wish I could tell this splendid creature that it had nothing to do with him, but I cannot. I feel impotent, then, often.

. . . not loving them enough.

Oh, never, you are their friend, their companion, their loyal one, though they are too busy among themselves to know it.

There was a blizzard that year. The youngest member of the family was caught out in it, not far from their house.

He got confused, his seven-year-old mind unsure of the direction in which to turn in order to go back home.

He wandered farther and farther away.

By the time the rest of the family was aware of what had happened, the blizzard was so fierce they couldn't get outside. They had to wait until the severity of it lessened.

The boy's mother was hysterical, certain that her son would be dead when they found him.

Hours later, the snow stopped altogether. The boy's parents threw on their heavy coats and hurried outside.

Over a mile away, they found their son, curled up inside the collie's embrace, in fact, so completely that they thought they had found the collie but not the boy.

They grabbed their son, and started off back toward the house. The father stopped, tears coming to his eyes, and turned back, bending over the nearly dead animal. Then he picked it up and carried it toward home.

The collie looked at him for a moment, eyes wide, heart beating faster, licking his hand several times, and asking—*I know, I heard him*—asking without words, but certain of a response from grateful parents—*Do you love me? Do you love me now?*

I want to pause for a moment. No, that is not quite right. The word is not *want*. The word is *must*. These poignant moments, tears and joy mixed together, these moments being spoken for those who will soon journey from the new Heaven to the new earth, these are preferable to the ones of battle. Spiritual warfare is that, very, very much that—fallen meeting unfallen in the heavenlies and, often, on earth itself. Oh, it happens, it happens often, former comrades contesting against one another for victory. Satan's plan is a multi-layered one; battles in human hearts and souls, battles between nations, battles among the stars, the astronomers seeing what they do not realize they are seeing, an explosion, a flash of light distant through the lens of multi-million-dollar instruments—not a world, like they say . . . something else, collision between evil and divine.

When my Creator has needed me, I have joined Gabriel and the others, out there, standing up to the forces of darkness— but, also, back on earth where the battle is not so spectacular, not between worlds, not amongst the stars, but in awful places, dark alleys, smoke-filled bars, theatres with flickering, obscene images, battles just the same, requiring warriors just the same. . . .

Warrior angels.

Gabriel is one. Michael another.

And sometimes Stedfast. Yes, sometimes me.

What is wonderful, truly so, is that the warriors are often able to minister as well. They go from their battles against forces of darkness, during these occasions, leaving the tumult behind, and perhaps quietly enter the room of a dying child, taking that little one into the Father's presence.

I remember once when Gabriel had just finished defending a group of Christians in Haiti. All the terrors of Satanic voodoo had been called against them, and he was summoned to vanquish the demonic entities. When that was accomplished, he learned that his next mission was helping some Kurdish refugees in Iraq after the government there had violated yet another international guarantee of protection.

"They're starving, Stedfast," he told me just before leaving on that next journey. "They are sick, dying, their bodies dropping by the roadside. Satan is getting at them through their Islamic fundamentalism. They have no hedge of protection. Yet, while what they believe is heretical, I must at least *try!*"

Gabriel was in great anguish.

"Oh, Stedfast, how I yearn for that day . . ." he said wearily.

"Yes, I know," I replied, "that day when all this will be over. The war will have been won, and our battles far, far behind us."

He was gone, then, off to the Middle East as a ministering angel—after that, surely the role of a warrior was again waiting for him.

I stood watching him leave, proud of my friend, and I realized what I did not often admit.

He yearned to minister.

I yearned to fight.

In those words should be taken no hint of rebellion against the will of Almighty God. I think, in such moments, that it amounts to something else. I minister because demons have caused pain. I minister because of the sin and the corruption that their master—and he and they are one, just as God and the rest of us are one—has propagated since Eden, because of Eden. I see tears. I see faces contorted with the effects of disease. I see people dragged off to Hell by his debased puppets.

And I want to strike a blow against my former comrade in Heaven. I want to stand before the collective demonkind and shout, "Enough! I am a gentle angel, I dry tears and sing away the pain, and give light to those in darkness—but now I am in battle mode. Now I am as fierce as any warrior in the rest of God's army. And I declare that you shall *not* gain victory *this* time!"

. . . our battles far, far behind us.

Sometimes those words are uttered in anticipated relief as my kind grows weary. Sometimes those words are uttered for an altogether different reason, as we emerge from the cesspool of evil deeds into which we must plunge on our various odysseys and are consumed by a passion, a passion not simply to minister to the *victims* but to strike back at the foul beings responsible.

I change when I go into battle.

I change a great deal.

I am no longer gentle. My kindness is a casualty. I am not seeking to ease suffering. I am committed, in a sense, to inflicting it upon those who brought the necessity of all this into a once-perfect universe, a suffering awaiting them that is of far greater consequence than anything they had been responsible for showering upon mankind.

Is that possible?

The world itself has been called Hell of a kind. And those who view it as such cannot be thought to be irrational, for they are correct. Can there be any other description that does justice to what is visible before one's very eyes—if those eyes have not been blinded by the master of deception?

I see, and I become angry, and, often, that is that. Then I move on to the task at hand, doing what I can to ease the pain of a hundred million demonized lives. That number is a modest one, considering the billions alive on this planet.

But I am not alone. There are other unfallen ones such as myself. Sometimes we meet on our journey. We communicate and commiserate and anticipate the new Heaven, the new earth.

"No more tears!" Samaritan told me once, thinking of what was to be. "No more absorbing their suffering into our very beings so that we can become better able to do what has been our mission for so very long."

The eyes confused . . . the flies landing on parts of the tiny body, the parts where there was more flesh than bones . . . the stomach puffing up with gases, poisons, disease . . . the last cry, "Yamma, yamma!"

"Yes, good comrade," I replied to this special angel, my thoughts becoming verbal. "And what you say is especially sad when it involves the hunger of a dying, malnourished, quite innocent baby."

"Ah, you are thinking of Ethiopia."

"No, I am thinking of the Sudan. I have not been there, but I have heard the reports about what happened."

"Of course! The Muslim leaders decreeing genocide for people in the southern part of the country."

"Simply because those people are not Islamic fundamentalists."

"A sad and terrible situation it is," Samaritan acknowledges. "I have been there with some of the babies, Stedfast."

"I did not know," I told him, with deepest empathy. "You must have faced such devastating sorrow."

"It weighs so heavily on me, Stedfast. Would you be at all willing to listen, my friend?"

"Of course, I would," I said, sensing his need to talk at that moment. "Please . . . go ahead."

"They are so confused. Their mothers cannot provide for them. Their fathers as well are impotent in this regard. So they lay back on the warm sand, and insects gorge on their blood, and the days stretch on and on until—"

Oh, how they change when they see me! There is a smile on each face, faint at first because they are still trapped in a ravaged body of flesh. But gradually the flesh is shed, the smile is broader, deeper, more wonderful. There is peace within it, lighting up their countenance. I extend my hand, and each one of the children takes it in his own, and one by one I lift them to Heaven, I lift them into their Father's presence, and He looks at me, and says the words that I treasure so much, so much. He says to me, "Well done, thou good and faithful servant."

"Oh, Stedfast," Samaritan continued. "We are hardly empty will-of-the wisp phantoms, just flukes of nature, as some will say—the unbelievers, you know—we are so much more."

I looked at him, and knew that this moment would soon pass, and the Father's enabling strength once again would take over. But then—then, Samaritan seemed more like a human child, looking out at the world around him, seeing the evil, the darkness, and not wanting to step out into it.

"As I go from one bedside to another," my friend said, "one battlefield to the next—and not always a battlefield of rockets and tanks. . . ."

"—but one of the soul?" I offered.

"Yes, of the soul, often enough, it is truly that—and I am dealing with a teenager who is about to stick yet another needle into yet another vein, and he is desperately searching for one that has not collapsed . . . and . . . and I whisper to that soul, I whisper, 'Stop, stop, you must stop,' and he hesitates, and I think I may be gaining a victory, Stedfast, I may be the Master's instrument in keeping that soul from the flames. But then the needle is plunged into the flesh yet again, the victim's eyes close, fleeting ecstasy filling his body, while bringing him yet closer to death, to Hell. They are so blind—Stedfast, they are so blind, and I have failed yet again!"

It is not difficult for us to be concerned with failure, and it is not difficult for us to think that the failure is our own.

It is not.

It is not the Father's.

Failure comes through the choices made by men and women every second of every hour of all the time of history.

People fail. Divinity does not.

Judas was the betrayer of Christ. Christ was not the one to sell *him* for thirty pieces of silver.

We know this, the other unfallen and I. We know it very well. And we know that when a soul goes off, screaming, to Hell, we are not to blame.

But we feel it, you know. We feel as though we have failed without ever having failed at all. A single question rears up at us: Were we not wise enough, strong enough, present enough to *do* something?

Yet there is one source of consolation for us. Humans have other humans; they have family, they have friends, they have clergymen, they have so many sources of comfort and encouragement.

But not us, not the angels who refused to rebel.

We have one source of consolation.

I smile whenever I think of that, whenever the demonic gloom threatens to overwhelm even me, unfallen that I am.

I smile because of what we have, because of where we obtain that which we all do need.

Where, yea . . . and from Whom.

How could we, ever, ask for more?

*R*ob me not of my joy. . . .

There are people who delight, it would seem, in taking joy from others and grinding it as dust at their feet. They live miserably themselves. They have seldom experienced a lightness of heart that lifts the spirit to levels of sublime fulfillment that are a glimmer of what is awaiting any who accept Christ as Savior and Lord, and, thereby, gain entrance into Heaven where there is joy unbounded, unencumbered by the sorrows of the flesh, by the twists and turns of moods that afflict every human being at one time or another.

For such individuals, those twists and turns are not from happiness into despair but, rather, from depression into greater depression, from a melancholic outlook on life to one that is near-suicidal.

They seem to be saying, *I am not happy; therefore, I won't allow those around me to be happy. I will enrage them, offend them, disturb them in any way I can, because in a perverse and awful way, I derive some modicum of pleasure from THAT!*

When people of such disposition are by themselves, at least the rest of the world can distance itself from them, as it usually tries to do. But when they are in a temporarily pleasant mood, and they meet a member of the opposite sex, and there is, soon, a marriage, with some children later, it *seems* that joy has supplanted the dark side of their nature or—perhaps, held it at bay.

Not for long.

I tried very hard to help one such individual, a man who was a prominent and talented attorney for the public defender's office. I on the outside tried to do so in concert with the Holy Spirit on the inside—and, yes, let me interject, what I have just mentioned *is* surprising. Can a Christian, with the Holy Spirit indwelling him, ever be so dismal a person as this one? How is that possible? Shouldn't the joy of the Lord be on the throne of his life, displacing all else?

The Holy Spirit has taken up residence in Albert, but He is not in *control*. This member of the Trinity is a boarder. He rents a room, He has the key to the front door, but that is that. Albert's sin nature still holds the deed, still pays the bills.

You see the validity of my analogy?

While Albert was indeed a Christian, he seldom proved a proper witness. Oh, theologically he might have held his own, he might have been able to defend the faith in corridors of intellect, perhaps. But where everyday living came into play, he was at best inept, at worst someone who repelled others from the faith.

Including his wife. His son. His daughter.

"Why do you think so ill of everyone?" his wife would often ask. "There *are* some good people left in this world. Not everyone is out to commit a crime of some sort, against you or another."

Albert's reaction to the latter point was understandably shaped by his days in court.

. . . *not everyone is out to commit a crime of some sort.*

"Are you so sure?" he would reply. "Can you be certain that there is not the psyche of a criminal in each one of us? The Bible calls it our sin nature. How can you dispute that?"

Yesterday he came to the end of a trial during which he defended a man guilty of murder. He was so good, so clever. He succeeded in getting his client acquitted. That man is now free, and may kill again, not stopping at one more victim. Albert, hired to see that justice was served, perpetuated infamy. Where is the justice in that?

"But there are good people, good deeds in Scripture in addition to those that illustrate what you suggest," his wife retorted. "Consider one of the thieves on that cross next to Christ. He repented. The Lord recognized this, and accepted him into the Kingdom."

"That thief had little choice. After all, he was at the end of his life. He might as well have."

"What about the Good Samaritan?"

"What about those who ignored the man that he eventually helped? Their number was greater."

"The apostles gave up everything for Jesus."

"Peter was certainly an apostle. Look at his threefold denial that he even knew his Master."

"But he wasn't a criminal," she pointed out.

"You're right. He was instead a coward. Is that necessarily better?" Albert replied. "A coward in battle can cause the deaths of his own comrades. So in reality, isn't such a man no more than a murderer as well?"

She became exasperated, as usual, unable to talk any longer, unable to break through to the man she loved.

Eventually she left him, along with his son, his daughter.

Months became years. Albert never remarried. But he went on to become a nationally known attorney. More often than not, he was assigned to defend serial killers, *mafioso* dons, discredited political figures, and many others of that caliber—though, judging by numbers, these types comprised the smallest number of his clients.

It might have been deemed inevitable that his personal outlook would become even more cynical than it was. Could it have been otherwise?

Yes. . . .

Albert could have refused cases involving criminals, those where no doubt existed in his mind that such men were not interested in *justice* as much as in manipulating the justice *system*. They merely wanted Albert to see to it that they would either never be punished for their crimes or, at least, get a much lighter sentence.

Justice has a price, he would tell himself again and again. *It is yet another commodity in this country, available to people with money and clever attorneys.*

The spillover from Albert's courtroom behavior crept more and more into his personal life. Though a Christian, he got further and further away from anything resembling a strong, Christ-centered testimony. The ethics of many of his clients subliminally worked their way into his own makeup. He discovered that he could make more money leaving the public defender's office and hanging out his own shingle. Soon Albert found himself catering more and more to these high-paying but questionable characters.

It was only a matter of time before Albert ended up being on trial himself.

For extortion.

It involved one of his corporate clients. A less polite word would have been blackmail.

He lost that case.

And he was imprisoned for five years.

Finally, after being released, he went back to a life that could not be reconstructed the way it had been. Though barred from ever practicing law again, Albert was far from being penniless. He had no financial worries.

But he had no one.

No, that wasn't quite right. The people he associated with were like those he had been with in prison, the same type, but not behind bars, men and women pursuing their schemes in absolute disregard of ethics and morality.

I am a Christian, he told himself one afternoon. *I indeed AM a Christian. So what am I doing with the swine, instead of being in the Master's house?*

He had fallen to the very bottom of the abyss in his soul, and he no longer could tolerate the cold despair.

My wife, my children, he thought. *Surely I can go back to them. They will greet me with love, despite all that has happened.*

But he had to find them. He hadn't had any contact with them for five years.

It took him several weeks.

But he did find his wife, his son, his daughter.

He found the grave where his wife had been buried. She had committed suicide. She had become infested with his own outlook, and this was spread to their children. When both turned to drugs, she could not endure the struggle to keep the remaining part of the family together, so she split it apart forever.

. . . beyond redemption.

No individual is beyond redemption until the moment he dies, because he has until then to stop rejecting Jesus Christ as Savior and Lord, and, finally, to accept Him into his very soul.

But some relationships cannot truly be redeemed. They have become buried, suffocated under a pile of harsh words and unfortunate acts. There is nothing that can be done to resurrect them, except by a miracle of the Holy Spirit.

That did not happen with Albert.

His wife was buried, and he stood before the tombstone on which had been carved her name.

I dug your grave myself, he admitted. *I placed you in it just as surely as if I—*

He remembered her face when she could still tolerate the sight of him. He enjoyed the feeling of her hair through his fingers.

Now . . . now only the children were left.

He knew he had to find them.

He did.

But what he found showed him the bankruptcy of the way he had been living. He found his son and his daughter in the same drug rehabilitation center.

"They are among the toughest cases we've ever encountered," one of the doctors told him.

"But why?" Albert asked plaintively, still not quite comprehending.

The two men were standing in a corridor.

"Would you come with me to my office, please?" the doctor asked.

Albert followed him. A few doors down the corridor, they stepped into the doctor's well-appointed, wood-panelled office.

After both were sitting down, the doctor looked quite seriously at Albert and said, "You see, they feel there is no hope for them."

"But what were they looking for in drugs?"

"Not hope, sir."

"What could it have been?"

"Oblivion."

Albert leaned back in the chair, his hands starting to tremble.

"But they had so much," he said, "nothing but luxury from the moment they were born."

"A fine suit of clothes is worthless if the one who wears it is filled with pain." the doctor said.

"Because of me—that's it, isn't it?" Albert guessed.

The doctor nodded sadly.

"Look at what you are," he said. "You have already admitted becoming like the clients you represented, absorbing their values, their outlook. Is it so impossible to understand that this is precisely what happened with your own children?"

"I don't know what you—"

"Forgive me, but I have to be frank, however difficult this will be for you. According to your children, if you saw a sunny day, you would wonder how long it would last, rather than be grateful for its warmth, its light *at that moment*. If you earned a six-figure salary one year, you would worry about the next, hoping your income wouldn't drop. If you—"

"—if I read of Heaven, I would worry about Hell. If I saw a smile on their mother's face, I would be consumed with the fear that an hour later there might be pain on it."

"Exactly what I am trying to tell you, sir."

"*But there are good people, good deeds in Scripture in addition to those that illustrate what you suggest.*'" his wife retorted, "*Consider one of the thieves on that cross next to Christ. He repented. The Lord recognized this, and accepted him into the Kingdom.*"

"*That thief had little choice. After all, he was at the end of his life. He might as well have.*"

"*What about the Good Samaritan?*"

"*What about those who ignored the man that he eventually helped? Their number was greater.*"

Albert glanced at the doctor.

"Rob me not of my joy," he said.

"That is surely appropriate. Who said it?"

"I did."

"You?"

"Yes, I wrote it during my college years."

"Why?"

"Because everything was going so well. And I became worried—"

"Dominated perhaps?"

"Yes, that's more accurate. I became dominated by the fear that my joy would slip away between my fingers like tiny grains of sand."

"And you guaranteed that that would be so by making it a self-fulfilling prophecy."

"My wife, my children," Albert sobbed, "sacrificed at the altar of my own insecurities."

"And from those insecurities were born a life-view that placed trust in no one, that portrayed everyone as evil."

"The Bible says that is so."

"How easily you raise your Christianity before me when it is convenient, sir."

"But it is what I believe."

"No, what you believe, sir, is not true Christianity. You accept the *evil* of others, while ignoring the possibility of their *redemption*. You have accepted it for yourself while denying its validity for others."

"You cannot compare me to the swine that I have represented."

"Consider this: How many of them, the swine to which you refer, and accurately, I suspect, have wives who remain loyal to them, have children who are loving and have never taken drugs, and who eagerly await the opportunity each day to welcome their fathers home?"

"I don't see the point," Albert said.

"That you don't *is* the point, sir."

. . . wives who remain loyal . . . children who are loving.

He *had* seen the point, yes, but he pushed it aside, not quite able to deal with it, not wanting to face even more pain.

"But how can they, being evil, send forth good fruit?" Albert mused.

"No one is completely evil."

"You speak as a Christian."

"I *am* a Christian."

"How is it possible that a mobster who may have been responsible for the death of dozens of human beings, how is it possible for such an individual to be worthy of anything but condemnation?"

"When it comes to family, when it comes to those depending upon him for his unfettered love, such a man was *more* worthy, sir, than you. What is the value of the gift of prophecy or tongues or teaching or any such gift if there is no love?"

"It is empty, it is cold, it is stale, it is—"

Albert could not go on.

"You *did* give them yourself," the doctor went on, "but it was that part of yourself that you would now like to exorcise. . . ."

Albert continued his silence.

"Do you wish to see your children?" the doctor asked after several minutes.

My children. . . .

"Do you *really* want to see them?" the doctor added.

I must. I must tell them how sorry I am. I must tell them that I love them, that I love with every bit of my mind, my heart, my very soul.

"Yes . . . " Albert said.

The doctor stood, and Albert followed him. The children, Martin and Julienne, now teenagers, were in a special section of the hospital.

"Constant care," the doctor said.

"Constant?"

"Oh, yes. We could keep them in strait-jackets continually, but that has its limitations. So we stay with them nearly every moment."

"But why? They're both locked up, aren't they?"

"You have no idea how violent they can become."

"Violent!" Albert started. "Even my little daughter?"

"Neither of your offspring is little anymore."

It has been a very long time, Albert, I whispered in my wordless way, the Holy Spirit prodding him to listen through his emotions, through a tap on his soul, a gentle touch saying, *Try to understand. Try to—*

"But you can help them, right?" Albert asked confidently.

The doctor shook his head.

"Neither will ever be anything more than a ticking human bomb, set to explode at the slightest provocation. Their brain cells have been severely affected by the years of drug abuse. And I'm afraid it won't get better. Brain cells cannot regenerate as others in the body can."

Albert's shoulders drooped. His voice shook as he asked, "You're saying they're doomed?"

"I would like to be able to put it in a gentler fashion, sir, but that is exactly what this amounts to, I'm afraid."

Albert felt perspiration covering his body.

I'm a Christian, Lord, how could this have happened? he whispered to the air around him.

That was my chance! He had reached out.

Because you have Christ as Savior, but not Lord!

He could not hear me in the normal sense. But he could sense something, something nudging his conscience, the Holy Spirit and I together in this. Albert could still be put under conviction, moment by moment by moment.

And he listened, to me, to the Spirit, inside himself.

Yet it seemed too late for his children, too late for their flesh-and-blood bodies as well as their souls. Surely he had lost them, lost them forever. He was convinced of this as soon as he saw his son, and then his daughter.

They were just human shells. They could barely speak.

All over the visible parts of their bodies, the flesh had sunk in pathetically where the veins had collapsed from constant puncturing, from the unholy wrenching demands of injection after injection, always a search for a fresh vein, a vein that could still do the job their addiction had forced upon them.

They had escaped AIDS, and that seemed a miracle in itself—but AIDS, as nightmarish as it was, could not have ravaged them any more than had been the case already by other means.

So thin.

Albert reached out to touch his daughter's cheek. She pulled back in that padded cell of hers and screamed at him.

"Don't!" she said. "It's so sore, Father, Father, it's so very sore. I couldn't stand anyone—"

Father! Father!

Albert rejoiced that she recognized him.

But then he heard the other words coming from her.

"—touching me. Please stop this man, whoever he is. You promised to help me whenever I needed you. *Get this man out of here!*"

Albert left, and went down the corridor to his son's room, which also was padded. The boy did not move when he entered.

There was no indication that he even knew he had a visitor. He just stayed on the floor in a fetal position, as though he were dead already.

"Son, son, I never knew what I was doing to you," Albert said, barely able to speak for the emotion that had been building up. "I was so concerned about the pain of life, the rotten people, the corruption—I could never give to you any joy because I did not have it myself. There was nothing but venom, nothing but hatred, nothing but suspicions, nothing but the darkness."

His son's eyes opened for just a moment, only that, and he turned to his father and asked, "But, Dad, the light—what about the light?"

And then he fell back into that inner world that had captured him so completely.

Albert thanked the doctor and left, stepping outside the hospital.

What about the light?

He sat down on a bench on the front lawn and bowed his head.

"They're headed for Hell because of me," he said out loud, weeping at the same time. "They're lost forever now."

A voice intruded.

"Sir, forgive me for this, but I think it is more correct to say that nobody's lost until God says that they are. Wouldn't you agree with that?"

Albert looked up.

No old man. No wavering phantom.

A beautiful red-haired nurse.

"I'm . . . I'm sorry," Albert said, his face nearly the color of her hair.

"That's all right," she replied. "Tears are cleansing."

"There's just so much sorrow in life."

"But that isn't all. You've got to realize that. You've got to grab hold of what is good and decent and loving and never let go."

"But my kids . . . they're here. They're dying."

"You don't know that for certain."

"But they look so pale, so weak."

"So does a neglected flower until it is watered. Your young ones are thirsty, sir, thirsty for *your love*. God loved you enough to give you the gift of salvation through the sacrifice of His beloved Son. You accepted this a long time ago. Why do you turn your back on the rest?"

"You mean the peace that passes understanding, that sort of thing?"

"I do. Exactly that."

"If only I could—"

"Your life had too many 'if onlys.' Give up this one. Banish it. Tell yourself, 'I *can* go back. I *can* stand with my loved ones. I *can* be the Lord's instrument for whatever He hungers to give to them.' "

"If only—" Albert repeated, out of habit.

"No more!" the nurse told him, undoubtedly louder than intended.

"You really believe it's not too late?"

"I *know* it isn't. Go, sir! Give them yourself, that loving side of you. Wipe away their tears. Tell your son about the light. Tell him, sir. Tell him about the light of the world. Leave the darkness in our Father's hands."

Albert nodded, stood, thanked the nurse, and turned toward the hospital.

. . . *tell your son about the light.*

"Hey, how did you—?"

He spun around.

But I was gone.

Ultimately there was victory, even in such a hard and stubborn soul. And that is something over which we all rejoice.

But another of my encounters during my odyssey shows victory of another sort, victory that is as wonderful, as touching, as grand as any I can remember. . . .

*C*raig wanted to be in the Olympics as a pole-vaulter. He had dreamed of this ever since he was a small boy.

"I pray that the Lord will make me strong enough," he said again and again to anyone who would listen. "I'm working on my legs. My arms are pretty good, but my legs need some work."

The family garage had been converted into a gym. Craig was there every day, after school and on weekends. By the time he had become a teenager, he had managed to break away on occasion, make some friends through social activities, go on a few dates—but, always, the *primary* focus had to be his physical conditioning. Few other activities could be allowed to intrude.

While pole-vaulting was the center of his attention, Craig proved to be a top athlete in two other areas of high school competition: wrestling and basketball. Even though he was a bit short, he nevertheless did well because he had a special characteristic that some of his many Jewish friends described rather colorfully in Yiddish.

Craig was young, good-looking, strong, popular. He had many opportunities for witnessing for Christ.

This young man was what I would have wanted to be if I had been of flesh and blood.

I was assigned to stay with Craig during those final months of his life. That sounds sudden, to say it like that, yes, I know that it does, but the Holy Spirit felt that this young man would be particularly sensitive to demonic oppression since he had been given so much in his life, and it seemed that the tragedy, from a human standpoint, that occurred had the potential to peel away some part of his faithfulness like a movie studio façade.

Satan did attack. He did not assign any of his demons. He wanted to devastate this young man directly, without any puppets, heaping discouragement on him, trying to break his will, waiting for a fist raised against Almighty God. He would fail, this leader of the fallen ones, he would fail, and yet he would not stop trying, no matter how often he was rebuked.

Craig was diagnosed as having a particularly severe bone disease. In time there would be not only pain but something else, a byproduct as much of drug treatment as the disease itself.

Craig's bones would lose their firmness. They would become almost elastic, like somewhat hardened rubber bands, and when they could no longer support his body, he would die.

One week before that happened, Craig spoke at his high school commencement ceremony. He was too weak for crutches. There was no wheelchair to carry him up to the podium.

A sack.

Oh, it was a bit more elaborate than that, but it still could be accurately described as a sack. His father and mother carried Craig in it, and then, when they reached the podium, as three thousand students and family members were seated inside the auditorium, his father held his son's head up so that it wouldn't

flop to one side, like a rag doll. Craig spoke, his voice so weak
that the sound system had to be turned up nearly to full volume.

"I love Jesus!" he said. "I love Him as much now as when
I first accepted Him as my Savior, my Lord. He wanted all of
me: my mind, my body, my soul. I don't have much of a body
to give Him now—"

As tears started to stream down his cheeks, and his father's
and mother's, rugged football heroes and geeks and cheer-
leaders and a very tough principal and every teacher in the
school shed their own.

"—but I won't have this for long, you know," Craig
continued. "It's gonna go. I'll discard it like the useless thing
it's become. And you know what? The Lord has promised me
a replacement, one better than the original, because never again
will I have to face disease or pain or even a cold. All that will
be in the past, over, ended, *finished forever!*"

There was surprising strength in his voice then. The microphone let out a high-pitched squeal.

"Don't go sobbing around about how all this could
happen, me a Christian and all. I never made it to the Olympics, but I think—"

He turned his head slightly, trying to whisper something
to his father. The words came through the microphone, "Dad,
will you wipe my eyes for me?"

As he faced the audience again, Craig was smiling.

"—I *know* that I will be doing something better in His
kingdom. I will run without getting tired. I will jump as high
as—"

He just couldn't stop the tears, he just couldn't, and he
was terribly embarrassed that this was so, yet through the
emotion, the remaining words somehow came through.

"as . . . high . . . as . . . the . . . stars!"

Craig had no strength left after that. His parents carried
him off the podium, and down the center aisle. Before the
three of them had gotten past the first row, the entire audience
stood and applauded. One girl broke away from the rest and

hurried to the piano on stage, and sat before it, and started playing, "On Christ the Solid Rock I Stand." Those in the audience who knew the words, and not many of them did, sang along with her; those who didn't hummed the melody.

Craig asked that they stop for a few seconds before leaving the auditorium altogether. He whispered something into his mother's ear.

She turned toward the gathered faculty and students, and, raising her voice through her own tears, she said, "My son wants me to tell you that he loves you all."

She brought a hand to her mouth, her own strength wavering, and in her mind she said, over and over, *Precious Jesus, precious Jesus, help me now, dear, dear Lord, help me!*

She lowered that hand, and tilted her head back slightly as she added, "Because Christ first loved him! And . . . and Craig has tried so hard to share that love with others."

Satan was there, though no one knew it except me. He stood at the entrance to the large auditorium, his wings drooping, his head tilted sadly to one side.

"You could have inspired acts like that, if you had not done all that you have done over the centuries of time," I reminded my former comrade.

"I know, Stedfast, I know," he replied.

"Can you offer anything that comes even close to what that one frail young man has done?"

Satan the Deceiver turned and looked at me, an expression of regret and shame on his repulsive face.

"You are so beautiful," he said with surprising softness.

"As you once were. The ugliness is of your own making."

He shrugged, layers of pus and slime shaken from his awful countenance, and then he went outside, observing the teenager's parents as they carefully put him in the back seat of the family sedan.

"I wanted him, Stedfast," Satan admitted. "I wanted to tear him apart, and feast on him in Hell."

"You lost," I said. "This one rejected your doctrine of hate, and surrounded himself with love."

"Yes . . . as with so many others, Stedfast . . . so many."

And then Lucifer the once-Magnificent was gone from that place.

That was on a Friday. By Wednesday of the next week, Craig's earthly life had ended. He died at home, in his room, the walls lined with photographs and certificates, the shelves stuffed with trophies. Every empty spot was filled with flowers.

One arrangement had come from his coach. On the card attached to it was a brief message: "Dear Craig, please forgive me for pushing you so hard."

Craig's mother, at his request, wrote a note back to the man. It read, simply: "No harder than the Lord, sir. God bless you. . . ."

People were camped outside on the front lawn, and on the walkway leading up to the front door. Only his parents were in his room with him when his spirit soared.

And I.

He was mumbling briefly, nothing that they could understand, but I heard his words fully.

"There really isn't any pain, is there?" he asked, amazed that he was at last truly free of it.

"None at all," I told this remarkable young man. "Pain is of the flesh, banished as the spirit takes over for those—"

"Jesus," he said, only a breath or two left.

Waiting for him at the gates.

"My Lord," he said. "He's holding something. It . . . it looks like—"

"Go to Him, Craig," I said with joy. "Gather your new strong legs and jump."

He did, always the athlete, jumping without a pole to guide him, vaulting beyond the confines of corruptible flesh and blood and bone, and reaching for the flaming Olympic torch that his beloved Savior held out for him.

*A*dam and Eve were close to God before sin entered their lives. Every human being since then has been closer or further away from Him in direct proportion to the extent to which they let their sin nature hold sway. Never again will there be the kind of spiritual union that once existed in Eden, at least not until the new Heaven and earth—but, glimpses, yes, there will be glimpses of what once was, very muted, even nearly nonexistent, and every now and then, much stronger.

Mother Teresa can experience a closeness that is not shared by a Donald Trump. That may be stating the obvious, but it is indeed quite true. This is not because of her works, for true spirituality cannot be built on a works-oriented foundation. Rather, her spirituality comes from the redemptive faith that has motivated her to serve Him in the only way that she knows how. When she gets down on her knees and says to her Lord, "I am giving You all that I am, all that I have, all that I will ever be in the flesh, and yet I wish, dear Jesus, there was more that I could offer to You," she receives, in that moment, a glimpse of what once was in Eden.

Contrast that spirit of sacrifice with another sort of spirit altogether, a spirit that is rampant in the Body of Christ, a spirit that makes demands of Him—prosperity, health—a spirit that postulates the heresy that it is more important to maneuver Almighty God into serving the human race than His creations feeling compelled to serve Him.

We should please God so that He will give us the desires of our heart. . . .

I have heard that, oh, I have, though I would have wished that I had not. It is part of the gathering storm, a storm that will sweep over Christendom, that will subvert whole congregations, though some members still may be saved, that will add the symbol of the dollar to that of the cross, the two intertwined in the minds of many.

When I see the flash-and-dash of so much of what passes for Christian service by the leaders of the faith, I know that the Rapture is not far off. I know that my Creator cannot tolerate the travesties much longer, that He must take true believers out of a world, especially a Christian world, that threatens to collapse of its increasingly virulent hypocrisy, pulling all but the elect down in the process.

And I think of the children, especially the retarded children.

If the adults around them only knew. . . .

So often, retardation in one form or another is given as a justification for abortion. Slaughter the babies before they enter a world in which they will be miserable, in which they will inflict so much suffering on others, in addition to their own— for isn't that the kinder act in the long run, the more merciful, a few seconds of pain, perhaps, rather than ten or twenty years of shambling disability?

If a baby cannot possibly measure up to society's standards, then how can there be happiness?

And yet the proponents of this carnage deny intellectual elitism! They scoff at comparisons with the Aryan mentality of the Third Reich. But their very words condemn them. They say it stops at the unborn and cannot possibly be a forerunner to eradication of the elderly.

They lie. . . .

Severely retarded children cannot lie, you know. They cannot lust. They cannot murder, or steal. But, most striking of all, they cannot deny their Creator.

A body of twenty years that houses the brain of a small child is that of a human being forever without the *will* and, really, the *opportunity* to sin in ways that are acquired through the years of the lives of "normal" youngsters.

It is true that Scripture indicates human beings are born to sin or perhaps born *into* sin. But when there is severe retardation, that *tendency* to sin is blocked off.

No such youngsters can ever be reached by Satan or his emissaries. Oh, he has tried again and again, but he cannot get into their minds, their souls. He fails each and every time.

And for the most beautiful, the most wondrous of reasons.

If those who want to snuff out these children knew the truth, they would never be able to deal with the guilt.

The truth?

I said it was beautiful, I said it was wondrous.

It is, every bit that, every, every bit.

For you see, each retarded child is in a state quite similar to what Adam and Eve experienced in Eden—but even more blessed. Adam and Eve went on to sin. Those severely retarded simply do not have the capacity to do so. Perhaps they will seem to have a bit of temper, but it is actually more a sense of frustration than anything else.

They will never strike another human being. They will never kill or rob or maim or rape.

They *cannot!*

A retarded child would never have taken of the fruit of the tree of the knowledge of good and evil because—and this is the wondrous part—he would never have considered disobeying his Creator.

There is a why to this, a sublime why.

Ones such as these have a bond with Almighty God that no one else can approach. If sin is essentially separation from Him, then they have never been separated.

I have seen retarded children sitting by themselves, laughing. I have heard adults look at them with pity and say, "Poor child! He's off in a world of his own."

Precisely!

It *is* a different world, that it is.

They walk with angels. There is no barrier between us. Unlike the rest of mankind, they do not have to wait until they are dying.

They are not lonely.

They may be alone. They may sit quietly by themselves and seem to be looking into space. But they are not looking into nothingness.

They see . . . you see.

They see a great deal.

We give them glimpses, my kind and I. We give them glimpses of the new Eden, which will be the entire earth. We run a kind of cosmic movie projector and on a kind of cosmic screen we show them what will be. They see thinking, reasoning, handsome adults playing with lions, lions licking lambs, lambs without need of a shepherd because there is no longer any danger.

"Who is that?" some will ask.

"You, dear child," I or another will say.

"Me?" responds a tiny voice, with beautiful eyes flashing brightly.

"You," I tell the child. "You, as you were meant to be, as you will always be in that fine day."

Sometimes they cry. Sometimes they just sit, uncomprehending. Sometimes they are scared and they ask me to hold them, and I say that I cannot, not just yet.

I love having the privilege of escorting them to heaven. Even as they die, they reach out to father, mother, brother, sister, and they smile, nothing more than that, but enough it is, a smile of love, of joy, a smile that says as much as words themselves, "Thank you for loving me. Thank you for taking care of me. God will take over now."

I remember so many occasions when I would sit with a mentally handicapped child and talk with that sweetly innocent one about what awaits him in the new Heaven, the new Earth. Mentally handicapped, yes. Spiritually handicapped, no.

"You will sing," I said to one boy as he played quietly with another child.

"Mmmm," he hummed in the only way he knew how, in the only way he could, since he had never been able to speak more than that.

"You will stand before the hosts of Heaven, and you will sing a great ballad," I continued. "You will stand with your friend here, and the two of you will delight precious Jesus Himself."

His playmate was also retarded. In addition, she had been born without fingers on either of her hands.

Her eyes told me that she wanted to know what *she* would be doing there, by her friend's side.

"You will be playing a guitar," I told her, "right in the midst of a whole new existence, first in Heaven and then in Eden."

She understood, for she held up those fingerless hands and studied them, then started crying.

"Mmmm," the boy put his arm around her and their heads touched, temple-to-temple.

He wanted to say a great deal, but the confines of the flesh gave him no words.

These two would be among the children caught up in the Rapture, and would not see death. I know the moment. Angels are not given glimpses of everything by our Creator, but this one He allowed, this one indeed.

Home.

They would be in their family homes, not in an institution like so many other children of their sort. The boy would be sitting on his father's lap, his mother running her fingers through his soft golden hair.

"Mmmm," the boy would hum as usual.

But his parents would sense something different this time, for he knew sooner than they, his sweet, sweet Jesus even then leaving Heaven and coming to earth and reaching out His arms.

They would look at their child, and smile.

And they both would reach out and touch him, each a different cheek, feeling the so-soft skin.

"It's time, Mother," he would say, turning to his mother, and to his father, "It's time, Father," and then to the two of them, "Blessed Jesus is here."

At that moment, they would be the ones without words.

Only a block away, the little girl would be in her bedroom, her parents in the kitchen washing dishes. Jesus the Christ would call her first and give her the fingers she never had, and a brightly shining guitar, and she would use it without human training, and she would call to her parents by a melody all her own, and dishes would fall to the floor as her beloved ones were caught up to be with her, together, taken unto glory, with a robust voice instantly joining in, the voice of a dear young friend, the two of them singing and playing to the delight of all throughout eternity.

Children. . . .

The defenseless ones, subject to the desires of another generation, in or out of the womb.

Children reach out so often in their lives, for love, for help in dealing with pain, loneliness, hunger. What of the anguish of a starving mother who cannot give her starving child the food for which that child has been crying all day, all night, many days, many nights? The child knows little of this. The child simply reaches out for the only human being he or she can trust, and even though there is no food in return, even though there is no water, the child sinks back into that deep pit of suffering without blaming the mother, somehow sensing that she has done the very best she can, and there is no more which she can provide. At least— though no food, no liquid, nothing but slow death—the child has love.

But in countries where sustenance is not a problem, where there is plenty of meat and potatoes and beans, where there is plenty of clear, satisfying water—children still have other needs, the need to love, the need to belong, the need to laugh.

*T*he clown had brought joy to so many bright faces over the years. Now, he had one more show that he wanted to make.

"I've spent my life out there," he told a friend who hovered over his bed. "I just can't leave this world without one final appearance under the big top."

His name was Sammy . . . Sammy the Clown.

He had given his life to his craft. He had embraced it mind, body, and soul. There was little else for him, little else he knew.

He was in the business of laughter.

He made little children laugh. He made their parents laugh. He brought joy to the sick and to the elderly.

He was the best clown there ever was, the most famous, the most loved.

And he was dying.

"I'm going to die in the center ring," he once told an interviewer for a midwestern newspaper. "The sawdust will be under me, the canvas will be above me, the smell of horses and elephants will fill my nostrils, and in the background I'll go out of this world on the laughter of the crowd."

"They will laugh at your death?" the other man asked.

"You don't understand. They'll think it's just part of the act because I'll be very funny even then."

Tears came to his eyes.

"I will miss it all so much," he admitted. "There can never be anything like what I do."

"You don't know what will await you on the other side," the other man pointed out. "Maybe it'll be something better."

"If there's anything at all. I may end up as nothing."

. . . *as nothing.*

Those words stayed in his mind, repeated in lonely moments after one stint closed and the circus moved on to another location somewhere else across the nation, times when he was looking out through a rain-streaked car window at the unfamiliar places through which he passed, at the strangers who walked by.

Sammy ran away from home when he was fourteen, and never saw his parents again. His brief marriage had failed miserably. But he still had a family. One brother was a dwarf. Another brother ate fire. One sister rode elephants. A third brother trained lions and tigers. Circus people—they were his brothers, his sisters.

"It's hard to believe," one had said years before.

"What's hard to believe?" Sammy had asked.

"That someday those often raging beasts will actually be resting side by side without a whip to tame them, or a sharp voice to direct them, and a lamb will wander by and see them, and sit down with them."

"You're dreaming!" Sammy scoffed.

"No, my friend, it's been promised."

"Who's the screwball who did that?"

The animal trainer looked at him sadly as he said, "Sammy, Sammy, Almighty God has promised this."

Sammy shrugged and walked off.

Sammy's version of Heaven was the big top. Sammy's version of Hell was anytime he didn't happen to be in a ring, performing.

The animal trainer would talk again and again with him about spiritual things, about redemption and damnation and the rest.

And always Sammy's reply would be along the same lines, if not in the same words, then in the meaning behind them.

"I've known Heaven, I've known Hell already," he would say. "Your religion can't give me a thing I've not experienced here and now."

"But, Sammy, you need to be prepared."

"You can't mean that! For something that is nothing more than a mere game played on the gullible? A few magician's tricks? You forget; I've been a magician as well. I just like being a clown better."

The animal trainer would walk away, shaking his head regretfully, praying for another opportunity to witness to this man.

And so it went.

Sammy had his circus, he had his family—the animal trainer, the dwarfs, the giant, the others. Most had been with him for decades. There was no other life, as far as he was concerned.

But Sammy started to outlive them all.

One by one, his adopted brothers and his adopted sisters died. One by one, new faces replaced them, strangers with whom he felt not at all at ease. Then there were new owners. The circus became a business; it ceased being a way of life, as it had been to Sammy for more than fifty years.

Sammy was losing his heaven. The alternative for him was hell.

I've spent my life out there, he thought to himself as he struggled to sit up in his bed. *I just can't leave this world without one final appearance under the big top.*

And he made it.

The audience really enjoyed Sammy that night. As he finished, a six-year-old child broke away from her mother and ran up to him, and put her arms around his left leg, and hugged him.

"I love you," she murmured.

He picked her up and kissed her on the cheek, and then, after returning the child to her mother, he told the crowd that this was his farewell performance.

"Ladies and gentlemen, I am a very tired clown," he said. "This will be my last performance."

A gasp of shock arose from the onlookers, and a chorus started shouting, "No, no, no!"

He shook his head sadly, and added, "I wish you all were right. But, you see, my blood is messed up. It's because of years of breathing this sawdust. It's like the condition a coalminer gets. Sometimes it settles in the blood, sometimes in the lungs."

His shoulders slumped as he walked out of the center ring and toward the back of the tent to the secluded dressing areas.

The crowd forgot him soon enough, turning their fervent attention to the beautiful prancing ponies and their sequin-collared canine riders.

That night, after everyone else in the circus was asleep, Sammy found himself tossing and turning.

He slipped on a heavy robe, opened the creaky door to his trailer, and walked outside.

My last night. . . .

He didn't know how he could tell that. It wasn't a premonition. The soon-to-die often feel the life force weakening somehow.

I startled him as I stood there, having assumed the form of a man every bit as old as Sammy himself.

"I . . . I mean . . . where did you come from?" he asked, his deeply-lined face pale in the moonlight.

"It's been quite a distance, Sammy," I told him.

"How is it, sir, that you know who I am?"

"I indeed know many things about you."

"But how could that be?"

"I've been with you more than you know, Sammy."

"Where? When? Stop these games!"

"I do not play games."

"Then answer me!"

"When you were divorced, Sammy . . . I was there."

"Did you work for the attorney?"

"No, Sammy, I worked for his boss."

"Oh. . . ."

"You gave up your wife for the circus."

"I had been raised under the big top. What was I to do?"

"She tried to live the life you wanted, but she couldn't. She wasn't emotionally capable of shouldering the burdens you placed upon her."

"But she wanted me to give up everything I had ever known, everything I had grown up with!"

"As you wanted her to do."

"But she pledged in her marriage vows to let nothing separate us."

"Those were vows you took as well , Sammy."

He turned toward the huge tent.

"That has been my home for fifty years," he said. "How could I just—?"

"It is but a thing of painted canvas and rope and metal poles, Sammy. Nothing more than that."

"I've had my greatest triumphs in there."

"And you will carry its legacy to your grave."

He turned away from me.

"Do not . . . torment a dying . . . old man," he said, his voice broken, weak.

"Your torment is in there, Sammy, not out here with me."

He became angry then, and swung around to face me.

Gone.

To his physical sight, I was gone, even though in spirit I remained.

"Where did you—?" he started to ask.

He was very confused at that point, worried that his ailing body was affecting his mind, as well.

Suddenly he felt the need to walk over to the big top.

His gait was slow and painful, but once inside, he looked at the empty seats, the "dome" of the tent, and smiled.

"My cathedral," he whispered to himself, lost in memories.

"And you have worshiped well, Sammy," a voice abruptly interrupted his random thoughts.

Three clowns were standing, together, in the center ring.

"How did you get in here?" Sammy demanded.

"None of that is important," the tallest, most garishly-painted of the three told him. "The fact is that we *are* here."

The clown next to him, shorter, less flamboyant, added, "You said this has been your cathedral. You speak the truth. For it is here that you have found your gods."

Sammy chuckled.

"You make more of my simple comment than I ever intended," he said.

"That is not so," commented the third clown, shorter than the tall one but taller than the short one, and with almost no paint at all. "You have given your *life* to this temple. You have fallen at the pedestal of your own conceit."

"Meaningless piffle," Sammy grunted.

"You call it such because it accuses, it entraps you, old man," the third clown added darkly.

"Please don't misunderstand us," the first one interpolated. "We are delighted, more than you will perhaps ever know, that you have done what you have done, Sammy the Clown."

Sammy felt a chill then.

"Delighted?" he repeated. "Why are you delighted if what you say is true? For what you paint is a picture of a vain old man who—"

His eyes widened.

"Do you now see a measure of the truth, Sammy?" the first clown asked. "You gave up your family for the circus. But you also ignored Someone else."

"I ignored only those who would come between me and my—"

"Passion, Sammy? Isn't that what you should be saying?"

"No, no, *obsession!*" the second clown interrupted. "It is not bad to have a passion in life. But it is otherwise to have an obsession."

"I stand corrected," the first clown agreed. "Your obsession, Sammy, has come between you and anyone not connected with this enterprise."

A gloved hand swung around, indicating the big tent.

We are delighted, more than you will perhaps ever know, that you have done what you have done. . . .

Sammy felt another chill as he recalled those words so recently spoken. He turned to go, intending to walk as rapidly as his old legs would carry him.

"It is not so easy as that," one of the clowns called to him.

"What do you mean?" Sammy shouted back.

"You *know* you cannot possibly leave this place, you funny old clown. *You love it all too much!*"

Sammy was scared, scared of the clowns, scared of what they were saying to him, scared of what he sensed about them.

You love it all too much!

But there, in that single statement, they had hit upon the truth. They had pointed out to him a singular fact of his very insular life.

And now that my life is almost over, what does it all mean? he thought. *I gave my last performance tonight. There will be no more cheering or clapping for me. What would I be giving up if I just continued on my way? I am too old, too ill to exert myself again. I can stop now of my own accord. It is not that difficult. I can spend whatever time I have left, quietly, feasting on my memories. I will no longer have to arise at five o'clock each morning to help feed the animals or to move on to another town.*

I spoke to Sammy then, after he had put some distance between himself and those three clowns.

I was not a clown, as I did, but a middle-aged man, someone who had seen Sammy many, many times. That was not a lie, you know. The God of Truth would not allow us to lie. Indeed I had seen Sammy often, though he had never been aware of my presence when I was purely spirit. Only when I became a child hoisted up on his knee was he able to see me, albeit in another form.

A flash of insight, inexplicable, fled across his ancient face.

"We have met before, haven't we?" he stated.

"We have, Sammy. You wiped away my tears."

Sammy's eyes widened with sudden realization.

"You were that little boy, weren't you?" Sammy asked, somehow aware, though not sure why this was so.

I nodded.

The little boy rushed out to the center ring more than thirty years earlier. Sammy grabbed him gently and lifted the child up onto his left knee.

"And what can I do for you, child?" he asked.

At first I did not answer but simply looked at him. Tears began streaming down the cheeks of that adopted body.

"Why are you crying?" Sammy asked as he reached out to wipe the tears away. "You are too young to be crying like this."

"For you," I replied through the voice of a seven year old.

"For me? Why is that so? I am very happy. Why are you crying for me, a clown, a stranger?"

Sammy's attention was distracted then, the next act ready to enter the ring. He took the little boy off his knee, patted him on the head, and walked off. . . .

"Can you answer me now?" Sammy asked urgently, never having forgotten that singular incident. "Can you tell me what this is all about?

"There is your answer," I said, pointing to the three clowns behind him who beckoned from the canvas tent doorway.

"They're evil, aren't they?" he asked.

"Yes, they are."

"Why do they want me to go back there? I performed tonight for the last time. What could they possibly offer?"

"They want you. And they will try anything."

"They want this old, dying, stooped over body? Why? It's a wreck. They'd be getting damaged merchandise."

"It isn't your body, Sammy."

He pretended not to understand, but he knew well enough.

"Why should I side with you? Why should I not at least hear what they have to offer?"

"Because having heard, you will accept."

"Accept what?"

"One more night, Sammy."

"One more night in the center ring?"

"That is what they will claim."

"But that's impossible. I don't have the energy any longer."

I looked at Sammy, his eyes and mine locked into a gaze that he could not break for a moment or two. My human form shed tears, just as it had so many years earlier, tears for the same clown, now so old and frail.

"Are you sure that you would not give up *everything* for one more night, Sammy? The crowds cheering, the music playing, the smell of the sawdust in your nostrils? Are you so sure?"

"I have already done it," he said matter-of-factly. This *was* my final performance."

"Only because you thought that it *had* to be, that there was no other course of action open to you, as you came face to face with your physical limitations."

"I can scarcely walk now. I'm far too tired to give even one more performance."

"*They* would speak to the contrary, Sammy."

"I don't care."

Sammy smiled defiantly.

"Will you join me in my trailer?" he asked. "There are some things I'd like to show you."

Sammy!

Shrill, insistent voices were calling to him from the big top, night-time sirens beckoning him.

Sammy the Clown turned quickly, startled to hear his name shouted in such an eerie manner.

He shivered with the cold, but he smiled at me again, though with much less certainty than a moment before.

"They sound so confident, don't they?"

"Yes, they do," I agreed.

Just listen to what we have to say. What can you lose, Sammy?

He looked at me sheepishly.

"Come on," he said. "A nice hot cup of tea can do wonders for the cold."

Sammy the Clown walked to the trailer, oblivious to the fact that I was no longer with him, for I knew, with an awful sense of pure-white clarity, that I could do nothing more for this old man, this lost soul.

He stopped momentarily at the metal doorway, turned, and said, "Hey, mister, I've got a scrapbook of my—"

There was nothing except the dust his arthritic old feet had kicked up, scattered about for an instant by a slight, passing breeze, and then gone altogether, as though it had never been, like everything else in life.

The circus tent was full.

The media were there, regional as well as national.

World-renowned Sammy the Clown had been convinced to give one more show, even after that so-called "last" performance.

Word spread from household to household, children to adults . . . one more night with the master clown, one more night with Sammy.

Three minutes into his act, he died of a heart attack. Three other clowns carried him off.

A trapeze artist reported later that he had never seen them before, since Sammy was the only clown that circus had ever had.

"Another odd thing," he said to the television newscaster interviewing him.

"What was that?"

"Look, I'll be the first one to admit how crazy this will sound, but, well, I heard some pretty weird noises, mister."

"Noises?" the reporter asked. "Can you be more specific?"

"Crazy stuff . . . yeah, very strange . . . coming from the four of them as they all disappeared outside."

"What kinds of sounds?"

"Weeping."

"Weeping?"

"Yes . . . weeping and . . . and gnashing of teeth. Isn't that crazy?"

End of the Odyssey

I cannot say how it is that I know but know I do that I do know.

The wind perhaps? A strange new wind from the east? Does it carry the echoes of hapless demons with it, as they realize they will soon be dealt the destiny that had been foretold for so long?

I hear cries, I think, from Hell itself. Somehow, damned souls know what is on the verge of happening, the event which they chose to ignore or dispute. They who turned their backs on the Savior—their only source of escape from what they are now experiencing, and *will* experience forever—their cries are far worse than any I had heard before, even as I stood at the brink of Hell and pulled Darien from it, cries not only of torment but salvation lost, salvation pushed aside and spat upon, and now they know it is as real as the very flames around them.

I sit at the top of a tall mountain, high above the clouds. The sky is without blemish. The world below is shrouded under a blanket of soft whiteness.

Another sound supersedes that first, that wail. This is different, and familiar. I have heard it often in Heaven my home, the sound of many wings—a million wings, ten million, more perhaps—beating together, wings of spirit, like threads of shaped mist, all coming from above. I stand as tall as I can, looking upward.

Most mortals below will never know, not those left behind. They will turn around and find a brother, a sister, a spouse, a friend, a co-worker *gone*.

They will assume any number of explanations: a gigantic world-wide terrorist conspiracy . . . mere coincidence involving a number of disappearances at the same time . . . some fundamentalist religious charade . . . on and on . . . without opening their eyes and grappling with the *truth*.

I see blessed Jesus now, coming through the clouds, His arms outstretched, a single word from his lips, a word that connects with the souls of millions, forming an immediate, irresistible link, pulling them upward.

I leave that mountain and scurry about the planet, eager to witness those precious moments of rapturing in every place that I can. I move quickly, before these have all passed by, before that instant, tragic and foretold for so long, when I must leave as a consequence, along with all other angels, leave those humans now standing in their puzzled unbelief, leave them behind in the grip of Satan more completely than ever before.

After a pleasant luncheon, a man walking from London's Simpson's-in-the-Strand to Trafalgar Square is taken just as he is pulling his coat more tightly around himself. He forgets everything, this man does, the chill London air, the traffic sounds, the paper vendor calling out the latest headline, the ancient odors that set London apart from any other city in the world. Yes, he forgets because he is looking into eyes, now, that are beyond any he has ever encountered, for they offer peace unimaginable in his finite frame, a frame that slips away even as the body itself is transformed, incorruptible from corruptible, words of joy escaping from his mouth as he is helped into everlasting life.

Helped into everlasting life. . . .

That is a description of what it is like in Heaven with which some theologians perhaps might well take issue. After all, as they would point out, those in Hell also have everlasting life.

Up to a point, I must say in reply, adding that being in Hell is hardly "life" as it was envisioned in the mind of a holy God, hardly life that is worth living. No, I would have to say everlasting *life* is only for the redeemed. The damned have something else altogether.

I come next to a Planned Parenthood clinic. I wonder how they have gotten away with assigning *parenthood* to the name of an organization whose founder's original purpose was to concentrate on the *annihilation* of blacks, a clever weapon to rid the world of as many of them as possible.

I go inside. There is confusion.

Babies are disappearing! Some as they are being scraped from their mother's wombs, others as they have been temporarily tossed onto a cold metal table.

Gone!

Nurses are screaming. Doctors are trying to calm them. Mothers recoil in terror.

I wish I could capture the moments that I now am seeing, capture these on video tape and show them to a society that *might* change its ways with such evidence before it.

I wish I could, but I cannot. What I see is for myself and, hopefully, for the consciences of other witnesses.

I see a baby who has been aborted whole, one who is supposedly dead, yet continues to live. I see a doctor order a nurse to "dispose" of the "thing." The nurse looks at him, and then at the living miniature human form in front of her, and she hesitates, wanting to obey her boss, the man who controls her livelihood, but not quite able to take her hands, put them around the baby boy's neck, and twist. Or shovel him into the oven on premises. *(Heil Hitler, eh!)*

Grumbling, the doctor pushes the nurse aside. As he is reaching for the tiny form, the baby is raptured—the baby is taken up, but not instantaneously. There is a transitory moment in time when he turns toward the doctor who would be his slayer, turns toward this man intent on atrocity, and, possessed of a growing wisdom, wisdom that stems from He Who is calling him, from that child issue forth the final tears of his brief existence, the last shreds of what he once was. Now there is only love in the tiny eyes, love mixed with pity—hence, the tears—love so supreme, so unconditional, so undeserved that the doctor breaks into uncontrollable sobs as he reaches upward toward the child, and the child down toward him. But it is too late, too late for conscience or regret. There is no more time. There is nothing for the child but the loving arms of His Savior and nothing for the doctor but the sharp talons of his own master as he runs screaming from the room to collapse in the corridor outside, not propelled by a vision of incalculable horror, but of a baby's blind, beautiful love beyond reason itself, a deep and total forgiveness he can scarce imagine, and never abide. That is why he can say only, "It cannot be, it cannot be, oh, God, it cannot be," again and again until the clutching darkness has him in judgment unassailable.

There are others in that cruel mausoleum owned and operated by Planned Parenthood. They call it a clinic. It is hardly that, for a clinic, as originally intended centuries before, was to be a place purely of the treatment of diseases, of the curing of ills. And yet an alarming percentage of what Planned Parenthood has dispensed is the aiding and the abetting of infamy of the most despicable sort—but wearing a reassuringly professional face with civil rights statutes rolled up in one hand and some surgical instruments in the other, with a mouth spouting procedures couched in innocuous words that taste like honey and burn the gut like arsenic. They are a Trojan horse of horrors, these human devils, smiling and so very helpful and more than a little efficient in the process, and yet deserving only the most pitiless judgment, the kind that surely will be served up to these vile servants of a mocking maestro dripping with the evil of himself.

The babies are raptured, yet the advocates of their "termination" are left behind to continue wallowing in their hellish practices, practices now become part of the fabric of a society, a world increasingly given over to the very same Prince of Darkness with whom they have been cavorting for so long. The Holy Spirit and all angels and all redeemed human beings are now gone . . . there is nothing left to stem the terrible foul tide.

Who said there is no justice anymore?

*I*t is nearly completed now, this my sojourn on earth, as well as the Rapture. I see others going to the Savior in the air. The elderly, once gripped by pain, suddenly find that it has left them. Those men, women, and children dying of cancer are taken, the ravages of that killer disease eliminated all over the world. The retarded have regained all their faculties as they reach their hands high, and He calls them home. Women suffering through the trauma that has followed rape are now completely at peace as they leave the ground, and He gives them a security that will never pass away.

So many. . . .

Millions are saying goodbye to sin, to disease, to fear, to despair, to loneliness.

To *doubt,* indeed that—in its place the reality that faith all along had been telling them was true.

True!

I have not seen True. Could my comrade still be there at the entrance to Eden? But why? Surely he must know. How could he *not* know?

I go to the Garden, and do find him as I had suspected, exactly where he was when I last left him.

"It is the Rapture, True," I tell him. "We all can leave now. There is no more place for us in this world."

He shakes his head sadly.

"All but me," he says. "My task is not yet ended."

"But there is no more need—" I start to reply, then stop myself, for I had been about to say, "But there is no need to stand guard."

He smiles, seeing my expression.

"You understand, do you not?" he remarks. "There is more need than ever that I, the last of angelkind here on this planet, be twice as vigilant, twice as strong, calling upon everything with which the Creator has fortified me."

"And you will need all of that, dear friend," I agree now that I understand that he must remain, what he must face.

For there is to be a wave of evil so intense that it will sweep over everyone who is left. Some will resist. Some will come to a saving knowledge of Jesus Christ. But most will not, seduced by Satan in this climactic bid for supremacy.

"I have heard them planning, Stedfast," True says.

He shivers then, as though the memories are shaking him to the very core of himself.

"I have heard what they will be doing with the living," he continues. "There will be more and more manifestations, you know, appearances by demonic entities as the veil between Hell and this planet is rent asunder. And mortals will not be able to cope. Many will be driven mad, you know. Many will take their own lives. Others will fall in slavish devotion to the new gods of this age. They will become as one with the evil one, and follow him on the path to damnation."

He pauses, then: "Devilwalk! That is what I have heard it called. That is surely what it is."

Together we shiver at that thought.

. . . *the veil between Hell and this planet is rent asunder.*

No angels to keep it in place, no Holy Spirit to hold back the onslaught.

"Pure evil, Stedfast," angel True says. "And I will be the only one of unfallen creation in the midst of it."

There seems to be fear in his manner at that moment, but if that is what it is, it is gone in a millisecond. And now he stands, his presence emboldened by a special determination, a divine valor.

"I can take it," he remarks. "I can take whatever offenses they fling at me, whatever foul tricks they might try."

"I will stay with you," I offer.

"You *cannot*. That would displease the Father, I am sure. He has given me my holy charge and I shall not dishonor Him by shifting responsibility to another."

True is being what he could never cease being. His nature did not permit disobeying the Father.

"I will come back, True," I say. "I will come back, and we shall walk side by side through a restored Eden."

For a moment, images of the original Eden consume me. For a moment, I stand there, anxious for the future.

I hear True calling to me, "I will be here, Stedfast. I will be waiting. Trust on that. Believe it!"

And I am gone elsewhere on earth.

*T*he last man to be raptured is named Jonathan, and he is very old. He walks at sunrise in a green English meadow with his beloved black-gray-white tabby by his side.

They have been together for sixteen years.

"It's a beautiful morning," Jonathan says. "Smell the heather, Boy-Boy?"

He thinks the cat can understand, and in some respects, he is right. This one does understand that he has spoken, and even if the sense of his words is lost on the animal, merely the sound of his master's voice is enough to set Boy-Boy apurring.

"It's been a rough four months, my dear friend," Jonathan continues. "First, there was that hernia operation. It was hard to recuperate at home. I still think they rushed me out of the hospital too quickly. And with Jessie gone, I—I—"

He hasn't stuttered for a long time. He did when his wife Jessie's heart failed, and he tried to revive her somehow, and cried out for her not to leave him. But that was a long time ago.

He reaches out and pats Boy-Boy, who digs his claws into the soft earth, a sign of momentary contentment.

"You were so faithful," he recalls, "always stretched out in bed right smack up against my right leg. Whenever I would groan with pain, you would look up at me, and it was almost as though you were asking if there was anything you could do to help."

This unusual companion had shown the loyalty and devotion of a dog. There was a great deal that Boy-Boy did to show his unconditional love. He would greet Jonathan and Jessie at the front door as they came in from a bicycling jaunt through the countryside, and fall down in front of them, and roll over on his back because he knew that that pleased them. And if they were pleased, he, too, felt happy.

When Jessie was in bed, that horrible arthritic pain constant for her, and Jonathan found it necessary to go into town to get a refill of some medicine, Boy-Boy would set himself on the pillow next to her and comfort her in ways that helped, that really helped. Once, after finding some relief from the pain in a deep sleep, she woke to find that Boy-Boy had wrapped his four legs around her and was resting his head in the palm of her hand, his warmth radiating through her, soothing her tired spirit.

"You mean so much to me," Jonathan says as he looks down at his side, and finds that Boy-Boy has crawled some yards away, and is now standing uncertainly, his legs very weak.

"*No!*" the old man cries as he struggles to his feet, and rushes over to the cat, sitting down beside him, and taking his friend in his arms.

"Come on, Boy-Boy, you can make it," Jonathan begs. "We've been together so long. I can't bear to be without you, too. Losing Jessie was so bad, and you helped me more than you can know. Please, Boy-Boy, hang on a while longer."

But the cat has no more strength. He had been close to death three times over the past four months, as a siege of tremors had racked his body, each making him more and more weak.

Now, as his beloved master holds him, he opens his eyes wide, and looks at the man he loves with all his being, and tries to tell him what he has just now seen, something bright and beautiful, sparkling light and music, and, yes, the woman, the woman he also loved, waiting, her arms reaching out to take him.

Boy-Boy's chest vibrates for a few moments.

"How can you be purring now?" Jonathan asks. "How can you—?"

Then the cat reaches out, and does something then that he had done often through the years, he folds his front paws around Jonathan's wrist, and pulls that hand closer to him, closer to his fur. How he enjoyed the feel of human flesh against him, and he sends forth for the last time a surge of warmth from his body.

But that is it. He has nothing more to give. His body sags as though with relief, but he is not quite gone. Some small spark of him lingers.

"I can't let you go!" Jonathan screams. "I need you just a little while longer!"

It is time for me now, time for me to appear before this old man.

"Let him go from that body," I say. "Let him put aside what is now of no use to him. It does not function anymore, you know, that earthly body is—"

"No, stranger!" Jonathan interrupts. "No, do not say it. It cannot *be!* I need him. I *do* need him."

"And your friend, your very good friend needs you to say that it is time now. He *must* go, for his sake. Release him, Jonathan. I know that you love him far too much to ask him to suffer another moment for *your* sake."

"But I'll be alone," Jonathan retorts. "I'll have no one."

"You will have *me*," I reply. "I will stay with you."

"But for how long? How long will you be with me?"

I am about to speak when he interrupts me.

"You have just arrived here. I knew Boy-Boy for sixteen years, Jessie for many more than that. Why should I expect a stranger to comfort me?"

"Listen, Jonathan, listen please."

He does that, he listens as Boy-Boy lets out a sigh, the body now limp, a slight breeze stirring through the soft, beautiful fur.

"I can't bury him," Jonathan tells me desperately. "My hands, my fingers, the arthritis!"

"It's okay. Just put him down on the ground," I say.

"But there must be a grave," he protests. "My beloved Jessie is buried only a few yards from here."

"No more graves, Jonathan, no more dying."

With great tenderness, Jonathan lays the still, thin body on the cold rocky ground.

I pause, smiling, and then say, "Now look up, old man."

He does. In an instant his tears are gone.

"You are the last one," I say, "the very last one."

Even for me the emotions are too strong, and I must stop. I realize that it is all over, this phase of God's plan for the ages, and what Jonathan and I will leave behind is not a world in which we could ever want to remain for a single additional moment.

"I promised to stay with you, Jonathan," I finally tell him. "I will do that. You asked for how long? I can tell you now."

"No need," he whispers with awe. "I know."

There is the sound of a final beckoning trumpet. No longer bound by age or ailments or grief, Jonathan is swept up from the earth, and I with him, beneath us the grave of the woman he loved for fifty years. Nearby lay a black-gray-white body as useless as hers had become. But above, ah, above, someone familiar, her arms outstretched, her smile the very light of Heaven's own radiance, and, waiting, at her feet, loyal, loving, beyond flesh itself, a familiar friend, a special gift from the Creator, now returned to them both, to be enjoyed again. No more parting, no more waiting for sweet devotion to be jerked away by dark death.

How long, Jonathan? You asked me, now you know. How long will I be by your side, and so many others I have come to know and to love with a measure of the love of God Himself? Isn't the answer truly, truly wonderful? Isn't it?

That is why the Father, my blessed, blessed Creator, called me by the name that He did in that ageless instant when I came into being, for it was to be the purpose of my life, the sole and holy reason for my very existence.

That is why I am what I am, and will always be, long after the lion lies down once again with the lamb.

Stedfast . . . as ever.

True's Epilogue

I watched that first couple go, their nakedness covered, their shame exposed. They left as a storm arose and swept over the whole of the earth. The first murder in the history of the human race followed, one son killing another. . . .

It is peaceful now. The sky is clear. The air is warm, dry. I await their return.

I have been waiting for thousands of years. Every epoch of human history has passed by.

And there have been visitors, human and demonic. They have stumbled upon this place, but none have gotten past me.

I have been capable for this my assignment. I need no food. I need no water. My sustenance comes from the Father of all.

I feel His power. I need His power. I am but one angel, and yet hordes from Hell have stood about, taunting me.

They have stayed with me for long periods of time, have talked about the old days of unblemished fellowship in Heaven before they followed Lucifer.

"For us, there is no boredom," one said. "We go where we please. We do what we want. We have no restrictions. We are *free*, True, and that *is* true."

I recalled the times when we walked the streets of gold, when we were in harmony, when the world below was untainted.

"You left," I replied. "I did not."

"To be in service to a new master."

"A pretender to the throne."

"The rightful heir—big difference."

"Deceit. Lucifer is the master of *that*, and nothing else."

They cannot tempt me, cannot seduce me into their perversion.

And always they went away, though always they returned, with some new taunt, some foul breath of deviltry.

Once, just once, it was Lucifer himself, not his underlings, not the duped spirits of a rejected Heaven.

Lucifer.

My once-comrade.

That is truly how it was. It was Lucifer, Stedfast, Darien, and True. Close in Heaven, close to one another, close to our Creator.

To have him leave, to have him turn into what he became was like wrenching a piece of myself away and throwing it into some eternal sea. But I healed. So did the others. Even so, we retained the memories.

And the memories were what Lucifer tried to use against me.

"You are lonely," he said.

"No, I am not. I am alone. But I have visitors. And I can call out to the Father anytime I wish."

"So said Another. And yet even He was driven to cry, 'My God, my God, why hast Thou forsaken me?' Remember those words, True. Remember them during those nights when there is no one, when there is nothing but darkness, and you are alone with the memories of what we once had, what we once were."

This fallen being named Lucifer knew what to say. He knew how to say it. He had, after all, persuaded a third of all my kind to join with him in his rebellion in Heaven.

But I was called True from the beginning. And that has never changed. My name is not Inconsistent. Or Wavering. Or Weak. *I am True,* and so I shall be to my Father, and to myself, and are these not one and the same?

Lucifer lost his veneer of propriety.

"You are stupid, True," he screamed.

"And *you* are false, is *that* not true? You reek with deceit. You shroud yourself with treachery. I serve the Almighty Father. You are the father of nothing but the foul deeds of your compliant demonkind. You stand before the human race and offer yourself as a messiah. Yet you are the very voice of Hell. *You offer nothing but damnation!"*

That got him, I think, at least for the moment.

Lucifer had no immediate reply. I thought he was going to leave, but he turned at the last moment, and looked back at me, beyond me, to the hint behind me of what Eden had become.

"Once so beautiful," Lucifer said. "Once so alive. . . ."

His voice trailed off, and he bowed his loathsome head as though regretting—as much as he was capable of anything of the sort—what he had wrought through the ages of time, epitomized by this dead, dusty, melancholy place.

Something happened then, one of the last remaining creatures made its way to the gate where we stood, a tall creature, rather like a young giraffe, born to be free and proud of its beauty, born to live without disease, born to last forever, without death to take it away into the dark night.

It had aged inexorably. It had become ill, contracting some sort of repugnant disease that reduced its colors to pale blotches and its gait to a pitiable shadow of what once had been.

Then it fell past the gate at the feet of its executioner, at the feet of Satan—and just as it died, it looked up into his face, and there were tears in its eyes. It groaned once, and that was all. There was nothing more. It was gone.

That was ages ago, centuries past. There are no more creatures left, the husk of once-Eden shriveled and ugly, and I continue to be alone. I have seen no demons for a very long time. Perhaps they have gathered together for Armageddon.

Is that music I hear? Has someone somehow slipped past me after all my efforts and broken into that which I have tried to guard for so very long?

I turn for a moment, to look beyond the entrance into that place.

I am startled.

A flower is blooming, looking much like an orchid. I enter Eden and stand beside it. I drink deeply of the scent it offers.

How can that be?

In a nearby stream, I hear the trickling of water over rocks at the bottom.

And swimming just below the surface are silver and gold fish.

Life!

I turn, and see green leaves unfurl on a tree that had been dead for five thousand years.

On one of the branches are two birds.

Singing! They have returned to Eden, and they are singing their joy!

A bush is green. The soil is rich and brown.

That music I hear . . . again . . . so beautiful!

I turn around and around. Before me, in an instant, Eden is coming to life, its own resurrection ascendant at this very moment.

I walk almost numbly to the entrance. I look up at the sky.

I see heavenly hosts descending. I see my fellow beings forming a glorious river of light and life.

I see the Son. He stands before me. He smiles as He reaches out and touches me.

I kneel before Him in adoration, my head bowed, my wings—

Two voices!

I look up.

Oh, Lord, how many times has there been temptation? How many times have I been asked by demons to turn aside? But I did not. I stayed, Holy One. I stayed for Thee.

"Hello, dear, dear True," the woman says.

"It has been a long time," the man adds.

They are changed these two, cleansed, as radiant as the angels accompanying them.

"Will you give us entrance, True?" the couple inquires of me.

I say nothing, I can say nothing. Words are useless when souls are united.

I step aside for the first time since sin entered creation.

The two stop just beyond the entrance, beauty surrounding them, life shouting its emergence in calls of living creatures from the trees, from the ground—everywhere are sounds and scents and rebirth.

They walk in awe, this first couple. The woman pauses before a flower of remarkable beauty. She bends down, pressing her nose quietly among the petals, and takes in what these have to offer to her. Then she stands straight, realizing that nothing has changed—if anything the garden is more beautiful than at the beginning—yea, nothing has changed, except centuries of pain, of disease, of turmoil for the entire human race.

"And all because of me, and my man," she says out loud.

But I go to her, more like Stedfast than True, and I remind her that none of that matters, that she has been forgiven, that her man has shared in this forgiveness.

She smiles.

"Dear friend," she says, "I said that not in melancholy or regret any longer but in rejoicing that our Father can forgive so much, that He can welcome even us into His Kingdom.

She reaches out to touch the flower.

"And now we are back," she remarks softly. "Praise His holy name, He has allowed us to return."

I leave them to their walk along familiar paths amidst resurgent majesty. Soon they will come to the spot where the Tree of the Knowledge of Good and Evil once stood.

No longer.

It is gone. In its place stand angels at their station, angels who, like me, will be with them time without end.

"What now, Lord?" I ask as I stand outside.

"Be with them, True," He tells me. "Be by their side, but not as the guardian of this place."

"But as what, blessed Jesus?"

I hear a chorus then, a celebration among ten thousand upon ten thousand of my kind.

"Be with them, True . . . as their dear friend," Jesus the Christ proclaims.

Sin has been banished forever!

I think, for a moment, of my former comrade-in-Heaven, of Lucifer suffering amidst the flames for what he has done, that for which he has been judged. I think of his guilt, his shame. But nowhere is there his repentance. It never came. He clung to his abominations and could not, would not, did not let go.

Then I turn and enter Eden, and, in the midst of life as it was meant to be, I think of him no more.

finis